The Roar of
Distant Engines

The Roar of Distant Engines

and

other stories

Sikivu Hutchinson

INFIDEL BOOKS
Los Angeles, CA

Published 2023 by Infidel Books

Copyright © 2023 Sikivu Hutchinson
All rights reserved

ISBN: 979-8-218-27030-8
Library of Congress 2023917922

Cover design by Alan Bell

Contents

The Roar of Distant Engines

FATAL INSOMNIA IS THE CRAWLSPACE between waking and sleeping, deep in a valley of occipital sludge, head knocking against the steering wheel, caught in the headlights of a semi stacked with American beaters headed for demolition, a goat's whisker away from being zombified, faking out death.

In point of fact, the zombies—skin scattered to the four corners—have it royally better. The condition is more likely to be misdiagnosed as something else. Chronic laziness, a balance problem, a motor malfunction, a mad cow bout, a smidge of dementia, an ephemeral coma; or, at least that's what they told Laz at her HMO. Swallow some of Big Pharma's finest and the world will be right again, the pill dispenser tech trilled into the drugstore cash register, ringing her up for more placebos. The disease took root through mutant proteins, wrecking balls trashing each stage of sleep. Up late, watching "Good Times" one night, Laz saw a commercial for a specialist. Board-certified. Office in an armpit one hundred miles north of Sacramento. Pioneered a procedure with a wild fungus they injected straight into the pituitary that zapped the sleeplessness. Brand new patent for 1983.

"We have one last appointment for Monday," the receptionist sing-songed when LAZ called. "Money-back guarantee, all insurance and benefit plans accepted. If we don't get you sleeping like a baby in twenty-four hours it's Vegas prime rib and a hot tub full of your poison of choice."

1

Stop. Think about the first lines of your favorite bedtime story. Who read them to you? Where? When? Repeat them twice, three times, four, until the words are an alien, animal language, wriggling on the spit of teased sleep.

Laz bought a Greyhound bus ticket to the armpit. If she was going to die, she would live in the throes of carpe motherfucking diem. See the state in one final blaze of refracted glory.

Five hours out of downtown, playing Solitaire on her lap to the tune of her seatmate's wood chopping snores, and the bus broke down in Buellton, bleeding transmission fluid in an apocalyptic river outside the town mortuary.

There she saw the woman waiting in a van. Sixty or so. Accent she couldn't place when she spoke. A handsome jawline that jaggedly went down to quiet ruin, Dodger blue baseball cap smashed onto her head. Rings clanking when she shifted gears on her beater, nipping at 200,000 miles. Laz could barely make out her face amid the hat and the gray hair nuclear fissioning around her eyes. It was the day after Ronald Reagan invaded Grenada. Six days after the country's leader was executed. Now Uncle Sam was sho'nuff gonna show those pinkos, swinging his dick like a Louisville slugger in the Caribbean. Protests happening across the nation. The Joint Chiefs tucking into their sirloin steaks as the island went up in flames and hundreds died.

"Where you going? I can take you as far as the Oregon border," the woman said. "Black lady by herself isn't safe up here."

A long line of angry passengers snaked out from the front of the bus, cursing the driver, God, the devil, and the bus company CEO, threatening to burn the cornfed fucker in effigy, Bic lighters at the ready.

"Me and the van had our birthday recently," the woman croaked, not holding out her hand or making eye contact.

The passengers beat on the bus door, chanting, "Greyhound can eat shit and die."

2

"Name's Amos," the woman said. "Used to make tools for an aerospace company down in Long Beach. Went belly-up fifteen years ago, but I still sell plane parts, supplies, do the occasional special order."

What, exactly? A wing fragment here, a cargo door there; the motherload being a metal tray from a transatlantic meal, engine lug nuts, half of an airframe.

There were packs of lupine white men roving all up and down the interstate, hunting for plane parts. A hoarder fraternity scoping out call boxes, rest stops, turnoffs, chasing wholesale deals on primo artifacts from defunct DC-9s, DC-10s, 727s. An elite squad from Barstow scavenged for plane crash detritus, hopped up on the thrill of decades' long investigations, cases crumbling into oblivion at the bottom of the National Highway Traffic Safety Administration file cabinets marked top secret.

Then there was a whole sub-industry of ghouls who searched exclusively for the crown jewel of a black box. Listening on ham radios for news of crashes. Hovering on the margins of airfields, flopping in junk cars whistling into the abyss, binoculars glued to the sky.

Laz looked the woman over. "Going up to Wynken near Redding. Can you take me?"

Amos grunted and gestured for her to get in. They lurched onto the highway. Amos rambled on about a black box from an L.A. to Wynken flight that went down in a golf ball hailstorm ten minutes after takeoff.

"Nobody could hear the black box pings but me," she bragged. "Those are the little signals they give off. Location detectors. Was born with dog whistle ears. I can practically hear fleas fucking. Been a blessing and a curse all my life. The little, itty-bitty voices and white noise never stop. Most of the time, I can filter it. Problem is, when they try and give me direction. That's when I gotta snuff 'em out. Let 'em know who's boss. Don't think you told me where you're going, girlie?" she asked.

Laz was no girlie. She was steaming towards thirty-five and aimless. Dangling over the mouth of a red river, viper-infested nightmares crackling on the horizon. She flinched at the epithet "girlie," summoning the wolfish once-overs of men jamming the city bus, the testosterone bombs who thought they owned the universe and hounded her on the street, all destined for unmarked graves.

Tom Petty whined from the van radio about refugees.

"It'll be wall-to-wall, I-lost-my-shit-to-Jesus claptrap from here." Amos snickered. "Once you get past Chino, the Christians have the biggest bandwidth. Gotta go through them if you want to sell anything out here in the boondocks. Come to think of it, I should've started a church of the abandoned interstate wanderers. Be set for life. What did you say you were going up there for again?"

"I didn't say, but I'm going to see a doctor. Office is a few miles before Redding. I got a motel room there." Laz felt her body cratering, stutter-stepping on the edge of sleep but not going over. Stranded RVs lined the side of the road, gas caps popped and gaping. A trail of empty gas cans littered the shoulders, breadcrumb style, all the way to the next exit sign.

Amos nodded, turning down the radio. "Just good to have the company at this hour. Just in case them highway patrol peckerwoods get a hankering for black meat. You got bags under your eyes, girlie. Night owl?"

"Depends on your definition. I don't have a choice."

"How's that?"

"I have this syndrome."

"What, you a vampire or something?"

"Vampires sleep sometimes. I never do."

"How's that?"

"Like I said, it's a syndrome. Ninety-five percent inherited."

"And the other five?"

"A DNA fart, like a coding blip. That's me."

"Fucked you up in the womb, huh?"

Laz grunted, waving away a fly that had buzzed through the cracked window. The Interstate five flies were big and demanding, hairier than the average bear, mega fertile in the bone-dry heat.

"Pity. Just so long as whatever you have isn't contagious." Amos smiled, resting her hand on the gearshift. A gentle clanking rose from the trunk as she took a curve too hard. "Let me know if you have to pee. I got these specially rigged waterproof baggies for long distances. Working on a patent for them."

"No, thanks," Laz said. "I got a thing for dirty rest stop bathrooms. Kinda like to get rid of my pee."

"In the future, the body will be totally self-contained. Instead of garbage in, garbage out, it'll be garbage repurposed into liquid fuel. Be able to fly Learjets and spaceships with it. Instead of peeing every damn three hours, we'll be able to metabolize, store up reserves as long as fucking camels. Take care of half of the drought-related deaths on the planet. It'll revolutionize long-distance travel."

Silver headlights pricked the blackness, scissoring across the windshield. The radio burbled out another world, Amos's prognostications swallowed up into a countrified rap song about forgiveness; bleeding into a spot for life insurance, bleeding into traffic and weather, tricked out by a hyper-caffeinated foghorn scat from an announcer named Brother Ezekial. Laz imagined him getting fucked between the Armageddon temps and the road closures, his lover diddling him softly in the control room while the Jesus freaks on the high bandwidths railed against Sodom, Gomorrah, and the Commies taking over the western hemisphere.

"Tip of the spear, brothers and sisters. Tip of the spear," Brother E chanted.

"He's my favorite," Amos said. "Feel like I'm about to drive into *The Wizard of Oz* tornado when he comes on. Ever see a police car ripped apart by a twister? Fascinating stuff."

They pulled into the rest stop. The next one was forty miles away, farther than Laz planned on going. She'd booked the motel for two days. All the money she could cobble together from her job selling magazine subscriptions and printer toner over the phone. The motel brochure had showcased a grip of dinky cottages, the kind of Midwestern antiseptic shacks that her parents had never been able to stay in steaming from Alabama to California in Jim Crow's gnashing maw.

Campers with Reagan-Bush bumper stickers snuggled next to the rest stop barbecue pits. Fish fried on a beat-up grill. A man kicked and cussed at a vending machine. Kids scampered in and out of the door of the women's bathroom, shooting each other in the ass with water guns. "Fuck that shit!" A woman yelled into a payphone. "Triple A says my card's no good. Can someone give me a jump?"

White faces flowed around her. At first, all Laz could see were her teeth. Then she saw a pink teddy bear pinned to her lapel and her fist banging against the phone booth door in rhythm to the operator's rejection. Raffle tickets hung out of the back pocket of her work slacks, the drab brown of a late-night diner shift slinging corned beef hash to eternity.

"I said, 'Can someone give me a jump?'" she yelled, lurching out of the phone booth. The raffle tickets dropped on the ground. Laz walked out of the bathroom and picked them up, handing them back to the woman.

"What about you, sister?" the woman asked, looking at her straight on, a boring, drilled gaze knocking down leagues.

But first, Laz needed to sleep, wanted to sleep, could taste it, sweet and teasing like the butterscotch ice cream she'd stolen from her baby cousin's cone at five, threatening to smack him if he made a peep. She tried not to look at the teddy bear pinned to the woman's shirt. She envied its deadness, the axe murderer button eyes that had taken some assembly-line worker one minute to make. She started to tell the woman her name, then thought better of it. Best to remain a blank. Let the teddy bear try and track her every move.

"I'm riding with someone," she said.

"You know damn well these white folks aren't gonna help me." She went over to Amos's van. "'Scuse me, can you give me a jump?"

Amos poked her head out of the window, chewing on the woman's plea for a second. She grunted, then got out of the front seat, grabbed some jumper cables from the back of the van, and walked over to Teddy Bear's car. The car sagged in the mud, a five-star Detroit shitbox with a Jack-o'-lantern grin grill that cried out for demolition. Amos popped open the hood and fastened the cables on the battery. The engine clicked, then died as Teddy Bear tried to start it, pumping the gas pedal between curses and cigarette puffs.

"I just need a ride to the next rest stop," she said, mashing her cigarette in the ashtray. "Got some folks to meet there at midnight. Got a raffle draw up near Wynken. The winning ticket gets—"

Amos cut her off. "Well, it's your lucky day. This girl here's going to Wynken too."

"I could give you a few bucks for the gas and the trouble."

Amos opened the van door for Teddy Bear. Laz slid into the back, grateful to let the old lady have the front. Uneasy about small talk. Eyeball drilling chitchat. Suddenly longing for the putrid coffee and burned rubber nicotine anonymity of the Greyhound bus.

The two old ladies were roughly the same height, stoop, and gait, Teddy Bear a little older. She cracked her knuckles. Amos flinched.

"I gave up that habit after I got laid off a few years ago."

"Goody for you. Me, I ain't got your willpower. Least not anymore."

A chiming sound echoed through the van.

"What was that?" Laz asked.

The women ignored her, snarling about gas prices and Reagan's Grenada fuckup, the wax museum sheen of Teddy Bear's skin making her dark eyes swim like buttermilk flies.

"Sold a mess of tickets tonight," Teddy Bear bragged. "Winner will be announced at the next rest stop."

They pulled onto the highway. Behind them, families waited to get into the bathroom for a turn at the communal sinks. Women schlepped dirty clothes, dishes, baby bottles from RVs, filling coolers with enough tap water to last the eight-hour drive up to the Canadian border.

"Look at that crap," Teddy Bear said. "Three generations living in their cars with nowhere to go. Selling any shit that isn't nailed down, carrying on right in front of their babies. Heathens. White ones don't get rousted by the pigs. Nice perk. That's alright though, we got Jesus looking out for us. You ladies ready to accept the Lord as your personal savior?"

Amos tightened her grip on the wheel. "Too late for that."

"Dumbest thing I've ever heard. Never too late. You gotta think of the afterlife…"

"Ain't no afterlife. It's taxes, serial fuckups, death, then dust bunnies for the worms."

Teddy Bear held up the raffle tickets, counting the leftovers. "You don't believe that. You can't."

"How are you gonna tell me what I believe?"

"Wait and see. You up on your high horse now. Try ten more years out here hawking airplane parts with no job security and no savings and see if you're still showing your ass to Jesus."

"I *busted* my ass all these years since I got canned, building up a clientele. Shit had nothing to do with Jesus, and you know it."

White men hagglers wagged their thumbs in the air from the side of the road, dropping them as Amos's van came into view. She rolled down the window, yelling, "I got tail fragments from a 1975 Pan Am and a 1990 Tower Air rudder. Competitive pricing."

The white men looked at her blankly and shrugged.

"Black box," one mouthed.

"Black box," another parroted.

Amos gunned the engine and drove on. No takers meant no food on the table. No rent money. No gas money. Stasis.

"What did you expect with that lot? Even if you've got cheap shit to sell, they ain't buyin'. Get with the afterlife," Teddy Bear muttered, smacking the dashboard. Barren fields tumbled ahead of them on both sides of the highway, crop dusters idling in the mud, deserted fruit stands moldering. "All this here's a crapshoot. Every second of every hour."

"Lay off it," Amos said. She nodded at Laz. "Girlie, I should let you drive since you never sleep. Be my chauffeur for a month while I do deliveries."

"Think of trusting Jesus like an insurance policy," Teddy Bear continued. "The more you spend, the bigger the coverage, the less the deductible. There's still time to let him in, baby."

She turned, flashing an earnest smile at Laz, and took a peanut butter cup out of her pocket and ripped into it, licking the flecks from the corner of her mouth.

Amos changed the radio station, sending the car swerving, the first peals of a country duet twanging through the air. "I don't happen to like extortionists in my pocket every month."

"Don't block the blessings, baby."

"I'm not your baby. What got you drunk on this Jesus freak shit?"

"Ten years bouncing around on my own after an eviction."

"How'd you get yourself evicted?"

"My, my… You're a sympathetic one. Sales took a dive. Rent on the dump I was living in got jacked up."

"And now you got a thriving career selling raffle tickets. Real credit to your race."

"A credit to the human race."

"What exactly do you think you're going to get from the raffle, *baby?*"

Teddy Bear paused.

"What kind of gas mileage does this thing get?"

"Shitty. But you know that. Don't change the subject."

Teddy Bear shifted in her seat. "Hated the eighties… Surprised the planet didn't already blow up around Reagan's arms race with the Russkies."

"Where we—where I am now ain't much better. Fucking one hundred degrees in the dead of winter 'cause of those flat Earth mofos in the White House."

"Fucking planes, fucking cars, fucking cows."

Laz raised her eyebrows. The exhaust fumes had gotten to the old ladies' heads, confusing them. The pink teddy bear grinned back at her from the second one's jacket. The car veered over the yellow line as Amos flipped through the FM stations, cursing the headbanging heavy metal trash, the Day-Glo sludge of new wave. A pickup driving southbound honked in warning.

"Watch it," Laz said.

Teddy Bear grabbed the steering wheel, steadying it, the raggedy transmission stutter of the car running blood, warm through their bodies. Laz examined the backs of their heads, their rhythms when they moved, the timbre of their voices joining in steely rebuke, droning into an evil twin lullaby just for her.

"Why don't you drive?" Amos said to Laz. "You've got a clean record."

"Squeaky clean," Teddy Bear repeated.

"How do you know?"

"You look like you do. Got that innocent baby face."

"Not a care in the world."

"Except for that minor inconvenience you mentioned."

"What inconvenience?" Laz asked.

The chiming sound rang out again. Amos reached into her jacket. The sound stopped.

"Ever wonder about those plane crashes? The last moment of consciousness before impact?" she asked.

"Become one with the hardware, the cockpit door, the refreshment cart, big mishmash," Teddy Bear trilled.

Clanking came from the trunk. Amos cocked her head. "Fireball over the ocean. That's the one good thing about insomnia. You never have to revisit shit like that at night in a dream."

The sign for the next rest stop loomed in front of them. One more raggedy black mile before the exit. Burger King, Kentucky Fried, Burrito World, Micky Dee's, all beckoning in operatic, greasy lust.

Amos patted her stomach. "Damn, a Big Mac would kill right now. Those cows have some kind of sedative hormone injected into them. That's why you got a McDonald's on every corner in the ghetto. To pacify the masses."

A semi pulled up beside them, mud spitting off its tire flaps onto their windshield as it zigged into the left lane. Amos shifted to the right and got past it, cutting the van off, tucking back into the fast lane triumphantly, a foghorn of indignation blasting behind them. The exit flashed ahead, ten yards to go. Amos put on her right turn signal, *ticktock, ticktock*. The semi accelerated, keeping pace with her car and blocking them, neck and neck.

They whizzed past the exit. Amos pounded the steering wheel. "Goddamn!"

The semi veered off the exit, clipping the fast-food sign, flattening the orange construction cones—pointing up like dunce caps—and skimming telephone poles. Sparks spit in the air toward the queue at the McDonald's drive-through, packed with revelers from a high school football game. They sucked the salt from their French fries, boxing the fuzz dice dangling from the rear mirrors of their Datsun B210s. Laz recognized some vans from the other rest stop, all lined up in a row. Idling. Their high beams were on, trained to one point in the middle of the parking lot.

The chiming echoed again. Amos put her hand inside her jacket and pulled out a square device. She put it to her ear and spoke into it.

"We're all here," she barked, punching a button on the device.

"Don't sell low to those motherfuckers like you been doing," Teddy Bear hissed.

Laz pointed at the device. "What's that?"

"A cellphone. Started getting big in the late '90s. Now it's a global disease."

"That's more than ten years away," Laz said.

"Bright girl. You always had a good head for the numbers."

Teddy Bear nodded. "Up until thirty-five, then, it all went downhill."

The two women drew closer, megaphone voices over the engine.

"Up until the accident."

"The plane crash. The sole survivor."

"The only one fully awake before the tailspin."

"Smashed her little self into the refreshment cart and held on for dear life as it went down."

"Took the trip in search of yet another quack to cure her incurable condition."

"Been hard for her to forgive herself all these years."

"Maybe a bedtime story will soothe her," Teddy Bear said.

"Once upon a time," Amos murmured, taking off her hat. A flap of loose skin stuck out from her forehead, jutting like a tab on a soda can. Teddy Bear squinted, reached over, and patted it tenderly. The flap widened into an opening big enough to slit a finger through. Teddy Bear sucked her teeth, fumbling in her purse. She took out a glue container.

"Here, let me patch your face up. You want to look decent for the audience—"

"Naw," Amos said, pushing her hand away. "Too late for that."

"I used to love Hansel and Gretel getting lost in the woods."

"Surely you're misremembering."

"Couldn't get into the little sequence with the witch being shoved into the oven."

Amos felt Teddy Bear's forehead. "Is it hot in here, or is it me?"

They fanned themselves in unison. Laz loosened the neck of her shirt. It was boiling. The velvety cool green of a McDonald's Shamrock Shake danced in front of her, teasing.

"Once upon a time," Amos said, "there were three women: me, myself, and I. Why do fairytales always begin that way?"

More vans were gathering in the lot, jockeying for parking spots.

Amos turned to Laz. "Can't believe anything she says. Her long-term memory's shot to shit. It was *The Three Little Pigs* we liked. I'll huff and I'll puff and I'll blow your house down. We always acted that one out. One pig had a house of straw, the other sticks, the other bricks."

Teddy Bear laughed. "Which pig are you?"

"The brick house pig. But I'm tired of protecting ya'll… Why'd you come back here anyway?"

"To see the unveiling."

A fat red fist knocked on the window. A white man with a gas can in his hand stuck his nose into the glass. "Hey, lady, you got any more tickets?"

Teddy Bear rolled down the window and yelled, "Sold out!"

"What do they win in the raffle?" Laz asked.

"A good night's sleep. Pleasant dreams."

Laz looked in the rear mirror. Teddy Bear was scratching her cheek, agitated, the skin rippling down in plaster flakes as she peeled it off like an orange. Layers fell onto her lap until moist eyes blinked out from a face that was luridly familiar. It was her own, thirty-some-odd years older, a frown scissoring down the middle of her forehead into the future. They stared at each other for a second, Teddy Bear giving Laz a tired, bitter nod.

"Now, why did you make me go and do that? I paid good money for that mask. It was the last one in the store that matched our exact flesh tone."

The smell of grilled meat wafted through the air. Laz opened her mouth to speak. Teddy Bear reached over and closed her mouth. "What did our mother tell you about keeping your mouth hanging open like that?"

"Our mother? Keep your hands off me," Laz said.

"But your skin is so soft."

"I said, keep your hands off me!"

"You're in no position to make demands," Amos barked.

Teddy Bear slumped forward, pouting. "Fresh and soft as a daisy."

"What do you mean, I'm in no position to make demands?"

"She means that you're due for atonement."

Teddy Bear whipped around, gripping the back of her seat, the raffle tickets tumbling from her lap. Laz glanced at the numbers and saw 21A, 22B, 23C, and so on.

Aisle, middle, window.

"Do you know what it means not to sleep for thirty years? Roaming in that truck like a fucking Flying Dutchman? Replaying every bloody second of that crash—"

"Quiet!" Amos rolled down the window and poked her head out. The parking lot teemed with damp bodies. "They're ready."

Laz reached for the door. "Who?"

"The listening audience," Teddy Bear whispered.

"What are you talking about?"

She ignored Laz and got out of the van. Amos grabbed the keys from the ignition and followed her. Teddy Bear opened the trunk and hoisted out a rectangular-shaped orange container. A crowd had assembled, their blank, torn faces rippling in the headlights, raffle tickets glowing in their hands.

Laz pushed the door handle. It was locked. She reached over the front seat and looked into the glove compartment. A wig, car registration, and insurance fell onto the floor. The registration expired in March 2015.

"So happy you could join us," Amos said to the crowd. "It's taken thirty years to recover this flight data recorder. Now, if we could have you organize yourselves by the rows you sat in before you… expired… that would be helpful. Front of the plane to the back of the cabin. Your raffle ticket corresponds with your seat number."

Amos steadied the orange container as the crowd surged. Mold, sand, and seaweed on their murmuring lips, sea anemone fingers digging mosaics into their cheeks, a bottom-of-the-ocean stench braiding them into a noose.

"Don't know how that legend got started about black boxes actually being black," Amos announced. The crowd jostled, pressing forward hungrily.

Teddy Bear stepped in front of them, taller, as though on stilts. She looked at Laz and bared her teeth, straight, picket fence white, sharp as a baby's. "There, there, no pushing. Wait until we call you. It has a bedtime story to tell us."

15

Rule of the Jungle

Do you, can you hear that sound? A ticking in the building. Getting louder in my head as I run up the stairs. *Five. Six. Seven. Eight.*

Don't tell me you can't hear it. The guard is one floor below, radioing for backup.

See, most nights, before my master escaped, before I went to find him, I was at the same perch in the kitchen window, watching all of you.

I liked to stare out onto the brown lawn of late summer in our trailer park. Watch it dwindle into a fire ant infestation. Pesky vermin. Not my kind of bugs at all. I preferred them fat and live wire. Insects verging upon reptilian. Water bugs, black widows, pregnant centipedes wriggling in my hands. Anything I could sink my teeth into.

My masters got me when I was twenty, I believe. My papers might've been forged to make me seem younger. In the underground market for rare beasts, older meant harder to housebreak, to coax, domesticate. Older meant deeper memories, battle wounds, regrets. The masters walked the rows of fresh-off-the-boat inventory, salivating over the smorgasbord. There were many other choices they could've made besides me, different body types, histories, but it was I who struck their fancy.

I was a special animal. Gifted with supersonic hearing. Smooth buttercream skin. High cranial capacity. They'd never seen the likes of me. Which is why I made my special, direct pitch at the shelter, pacing the floor of my cage seductively, giving the female of the species a deep, fluffy gaze, tossing the male of the species a hard stare; divide and conquer, flatter and repel. Yes, I was the envy of my fellow inmates. They were white hot with longing when I bid them farewell.

Of course, I wanted to be loyal to the masters. To be the *bestest*, the *mostest*, the premiere beast in the jungle, aching to be stroked, to be seen.

After they moved me in, I noticed certain things about the male. His gun collection, his preening in the mirror, the way he paraded around naked so I could see him in all his furry glory. He was building something, he bragged, patting me under the chin as he pried open my back, inserting, connecting wires. You don't understand me, he said, not knowing how wrong he was. See, in the shelter, I'd mastered their language: the syntax, grammar, turns of phrase. Schooled by another beast who'd lived among them for a while.

At night, my masters argued. Ripping each other apart about the light bill, the toilet seat being up, the panhandling she did at the gas station, the time she spent away from home looking for jobs. The map he was drawing at all hours, crammed into the bathroom with a case of beer on his knees.

The map said something about Revelation, a chapter from this big, raggedy black book he quoted from. Carried one in his pocket to work installing cold machines called air conditioners.

We had an air conditioner in the trailer, but it broke down that summer. Even they couldn't fix it. It kept babbling out numbers and things, what they called future predictions. They banged on it and told it to shut the fuck up, then junked it when it didn't obey. I felt sorry for it. But it didn't know the rule of the jungle. Have a purpose or be exterminated.

See, master said the sun was going to burn out one day. The government would shoot it right through the heart. *Kersplat.*

The black book told him so. He said he snuck and read it on service calls, working in this federal building place repairing the cold machines. When he took me between his legs to calm himself after a long day, I could feel the rage thrumming through him.

I'd always get fed wonderfully afterward. Not the usual dried-up Kibbles 'n Bits or table scraps, but calcium packed stuff. A femur here. A tibia there. Memorabilia from his travels.

The sound started then. I woke up one morning, and it was there. Ticking low as a dog whistle. A hippocampus pinprick, getting louder.

Can you hear it? Tell me you can.

I digress. I saw lots of things from my perch above the kitchen sink. Pods my masters called families doing their business, moving things in and out of their campers. Early in the morning, other families replaced them. Parasites who couldn't pay their rent, he growled. He was late for work and yelped at the female over the money they owed the taxman, always picking our pockets. Shit-eating vultures, he spat at them on the phone. Collection calls flooding them, noon and night.

When our water got shut off, master took some from the neighbor's hose. Softly. Cutting through the bushes so as not to wake them up, squirting it into the big pot he used to boil meat in, a smell that took over the whole camper.

One day, the female just up and left because of it. Or was it due to how close he and I became, like we could read each other's minds, kin to each other? In his room, I'd straddle his leg and lick his gunpowder fingers, listen to the bubbling on the stove like a lullaby.

When the gas company came to cut the heat off, he marched into the courtyard, rebel yelling to the moon and stars about how he'd defend the fort against interlopers.

Are you sure you can't hear it? The ticking?

After she left, the days stretched out longer. I'd wait for his return, bracing at the door for the pitter-patter of paws as he came back from his meetings with the other masters he called patriots. At night, he tossed and turned in his bulletproof vest, talking in his sleep about chasing birds, the exact layout of the third-floor office where the boss sat on his ass, barking out orders to the underlings. They got a hair more than minimum wage, installing cold machines from sea to shining sea, he said, holding me close, whispering about our destiny, a brass knuckle fist closing over his brain.

I kept watch over him until he woke up. Never straying. Except for once… to check to see if the cold machine was really gone. No, no, I couldn't have rivals. *Tick. Tick. Tick.*

He'd follow the boss home. At first, accidentally getting off on the same exit, tailing him 'til he got to his cul-de-sac. Sitting in front of his big old brick house with three gables and a chimney that belched out all the evil he did to the rank-and-file pups grinding their eight bucks an hour down to dust.

I knew every inch of the office building from the map he showed me. How every cubicle and trash can was arranged. The dusty, rusty water in the hall fountains, the death march of every wall clock, the urinal chitchat about football, the carnal knowledge they were losing their minds over, pissing on god and the holy black book, he said.

I waited up for him later and later, the food in my bowl down to scraps. I got so hungry I saw double. There was another beast-in-waiting, just like me, in a kitchen window across the courtyard. Same nose, same fingers, same lips, same slithery eyes, preparing for a long night at the foot of master's bed. His smell on its teeth.

One morning, they came with padlocks and a chain-link fence. I rushed them the way master had taught me, biting their knees, growling like a whole beast army. Doing him proud.

Except, he didn't come back that night or the next. I kept watch over the bed in the dark. Put the female's personal effects in the trash can for good. Waited. The sound roaring in me.

I went out to find him. Tracking his scent all the way to the office complex, through the backstreets, the signposts so familiar, even though they were in this mutt language, and the traffic sounds were making my ears bleed. I dropped on all fours, barely skittered past the guards in security, up, up the stairs, everything just like master's maps, down to a T. The sound drowned out the guard's command to stop. Up, up over the tap of keyboards, printers, pink slips. Up, up to the lair of master's boss, and my skin is tingling now. But I don't see master among all the other slaving mutts.

He'd told me we'd always be together. He'd lied. Cross your heart and hope to die, he'd whispered. All along, he'd been crafting a special mission that could make us immortal at the same time, master and beast, paw in hand. No boundary, no difference, never to be underestimated or separated again.

Except, master is nowhere to be found. And the ticking is in my chest now, a fledgling coming into its own in the moonlight, sinking its fangs into the building, rooting out the Lucifers who did master wrong.

If I could grow a tail like his in half a second, I could reach around, disable the bomb he planted under my vertebrae. Put it to sleep, settle back to watching you from my perch in the window.

All you good citizens, soft, oblivious. Gloriously dead to the world in your routines.

Passing Days

SITTING AT THE CAFÉ TABLE, trying to stretch the last two dollars of her paycheck, she played the game of firsts. Duos, trios, quartets dawdled by. A crush of humans. Every imaginable shape, color, and size unfurled on a reeking silver platter. Tower of Babel families. Groping, grasping heteros. Jocks and office workers, and idlers and pinstripe-suited men looking like closet pyros, waiting in line for caffeine bombs and the joy of seeing their names scribbled on paper cups.

She'd been fired from her mini-mart job the week before. Caught stealing from the cash register. Front row and center on the jumpy surveillance video playback, the boss agreeing to dump her without calling the cops if she forfeited a month's pay. Didn't steal anything, and didn't consent to be a slave for you, she'd screamed at him in all caps in her head on the way out.

In her head, the theft was operatic. Robin Hood barreling into the sunset, saving orphans from pimp priests. On the train ride home, she choreographed revenge on the boss, down to the minutest detail. Vowing to go back with red paint and a blowtorch to burn the sanctimony from his blubbery body. Telling no one in the sublet she shared with three other fitfully employed drifters who peeled dry skin between their toes for fun. She'd hit them up for loans one too many times, woke up with an eviction notice taped to her headboard.

Well, fuck them down to the Stygian studs of hell.

She swigged from a container of mouthwash, gargled, and spat into the cup with her human name on it. Took out her sketch pad and started drawing an ark. Configuring the walls, floor, and deck, the cargo space for the animals. Four-legged beasts, winged beasts, human beasts. Wild things who would all have to find a way to survive together, coexist peacefully in a floating sliver of time and space. If she finished before the backstories overtook her, she could live there. If she finished before the Gorgon waves of infected memories knocked her down, spirited her away, she'd be safe from them all.

Summer was bursting everywhere. Convertibles chugging in and out of the parking lot. Rat boys festering under tight cotton tank tops. She leaned back in her chair, concentrated, played firsts with a pair of chichi Westside breeders sporting matching blood diamonds on their fingers.

Their blond spawn teetered between the male's legs. She caught his eye and grinned. He grinned back, goofily, a floppy-eared puppy in a pet store window. She took out her toy Captain Crunch cereal box Yo-Yo and flashed it at him. Collect all five, lime green to aqua, and be king for life, the ad on the box had teased.

The spawn giggled and held out his hand.

"Don't be greedy, James," the heteros said in near unison.

She handed him the Yo-Yo. He studied it, cramming it in his mouth. The woman shrieked and hissed at her, clawing the Yo-Yo from between his lips and throwing it on the ground.

"What were you thinking? He could've choked!"

She looked through the woman and said nothing, shading in a pirate's flag on the ark. Her partner wagged his finger and frowned. "Not really."

"What do you mean, 'not really'?" The man grabbed the boy's hand tightly, whispering in his moist ear.

Briony walked to the bathroom. The man followed her. "Smart ass," he spat.

She turned, daring him to take another step. "He's first. You're second."

"Cute. Whatever the fuck you're saying."

Who'd be the first to die out of a pair? Pick a pair, any pair, at random; then go. Humans, jostled together on a street corner, fidgeting behind a rush-hour bus window, comatose in an office staff meeting, nuzzling up in a post-coital sludge of doubt, dawdling disgust. Humans in endless yawning, shuffling, wishing, hungering, math bucking, dancing on the head of pin configurations. Too many to document.

The game of firsts began after the accident. A rebuke to the clock's minute hand, lying in her hospital bed, waiting for the doctor's umpteenth prognosis on her condition. Her father said she'd been in a car crash, reveling in reconstructing it frame by frame, from impact to oblivion. Crowing about how it was a miracle she'd survived, a triumph of modern medicine, good genes, marathon prayers from all the strangers who'd heard about the bashed-up girl who'd lost a chunk of her brain on a slick freeway overpass.

Every morning when she woke up, her memories had been hijacked by his retelling. In one, she was learning how to drive and lost control. In two, jackhammer tractor trailers clipped them. In three, a slow, pea soup fog descended, smacking them into the center divider. Three doors, three cliffhangers trotted out between IVs as the nurses pumped her full of painkillers and shot her to the moon on a silver rocket, each hour a cyclone of drugs and needles, lukewarm green Jell-O cups for breakfast, lunch, and dinner; police detectives hovering over her, trying to piece together an incident report from her father's pack of lies absolving him of blame for the matter of her stranded body, the alien face staring back at her, tossing, turning, an ocean away.

A week after she arrived, a surgeon glided in, whispering in a soul falsetto that she was a good candidate for a made-in-America face transplant. The procedure would take under an hour. Johnny be nimble, Johnny be quick. They had performed only one hundred in the world. A simple installment plan. A sheath of synthetic material grafted onto the hardware of her bones, and, voilà; she'd be part of a secret society of phoenixes.

Recovering afterward, she'd listened to the churn of her roommate's oxygen monitor, watched their next of kin slouch in and out, veering from agonized to hopeful to euphoric that it wasn't them buried under a phalanx of wires. Hemming and hawing and handwringing and pleading and bargaining with god and the devil over the less than epic life story of the soon-to-be dearly departed. Secretly chewing on their luck their own niggling little countdown to worm-and-dust-mite snack food hadn't crashed and burned.

Yet.

A barista came through the café, clearing trash, giving Briony the once-over with buttery eyes.

"Tables are for paying customers," she chirped.

Briony pointed to her empty cup. "Just got out of the hospital."

The barista swept dirty napkins and a used Metro card into her garbage bag. "Sorry to hear it."

"Big accident. Multiple surgeries. Out of work for weeks."

She nodded and kept moving, impervious to the sympathy play.

"A face transplant, in fact."

The woman flinched, tightening her grip on the bag.

"Here, feel," Briony said, turning her cheek to the light. "Soft as a baby's bottom." She leaned in toward the barista, knocked back by the sweat tang rising from her shaggy blond pits.

"Nah, I'll take your word for it."

"I can hook you up with one if you want."

"You're nuts."

"Insurance doesn't cover it. The government has a special fund for them, though. I was one of the first recipients."

"Stop shitting me."

"Serious as a heart attack."

"What's the copay for minions like us?"

"Chump change."

"Shitting me for sure. Everybody would be doing it then. Pop in for an outpatient procedure, then *wham*. Heard you can change the features at will, with a thought or something. Like, if you were looking at someone… That true?"

Briony paused. "I'm thinking about you. See any change?"

"No. What were you thinking?"

"How long have you worked here?"

"Long. Just made assistant manager."

"Sweet. Hope that's a nice bump."

"Nonunion. Only so far we can go. These dumb shits gotta get it together and organize, not be so afraid of their own shadows."

"That's probably the greatest thing to be afraid of."

"Got a point there. Especially when you have skin in the game and there's principle and fear involved." She paused, brushing Briony's cheek with her knuckles. "Impressive."

"What'd I tell you? Baby's ass."

"How long it take you to heal?"

"From the surgery? Don't remember any of it."

"Oh, yeah? Lucky you."

"The humans remember the physical shit."

The barista looked her up and down, gathered up the trash bag, bemusement playing on her lips. "The *humans* remember… Is that so? I'd like to get me some of that kind of amnesia."

"Naw, there are side effects."

27

Side effects. Specifically—tremors, voices nibbling on the edges of her body, as she is strung out across time zones and brownfields, tossing and turning in the maw of the 7 a.m. alarm in a cold sweat about finding another job. One that paid enough for her to make rent, stay fed, keep the goblins and creditors at bay.

The longest job she ever had was cleaning fish on the river dock by the bridge, near the apartment she squatted in for five years. Most of the other local kids only lasted a few days. They fumbled and bumbled, then quit midweek, worn down by the smell, the slime, the blood. Briony hadn't minded the trio of horrors. She plunged her knife into the fish carcasses, scraping the scales, dispatching the limp beasts lovingly into a nice ice bath with other gutted travelers. At the end of the day, the docks were full to the brim with vats of fish eyes ready for the city dump. She daydreamed of tracing back their sight to the beginning. The wriggling from the egg out into the void of the sea. The swimming, resting, eating, breeding. The relentless plod to death in a predator's gut, ambushed by parasites, speared at the end of a hook. She jonesed for the oracular power of fish eyes, envying them lying there under her thumb, at peace. She could outlast, outskin, outscale the most crackerjack lifer, working at warp speed for a few more nickels; a simple trick of projecting herself onto the other side of the dock, onto passing barges and skiffs, below the coke-smeared decks of Wall Street luxury yachts to furtive spirit fucks and bodies thrown overboard, disintegrating upon contact. She thought of all the forensics on the bottom of the river eluding capture. Could hear the primordial hum of microscopic bone fragments, homicides, and suicides, and accidents commingling in beer cans and trash bags. She told her father about it and got slapped. Openhanded, the underside of his pinkie ring just missing her eyelid.

He died behind the wheel of his Buick Regal, waiting to score some coke at a stoplight. The autopsy was inconclusive. Heart attack, aneurysm, seizure, OD, natural causes. A smorgasbord of proposed maladies. His funeral obit screamed that he'd been cut down in the prime of life. A pioneering freeway engineer who held the city in his palm. A white-passing fraud who'd spent donkey's years designing overpasses that scissored through ghettos, reborn into gleaming citadels for robber barons. Hours before he croaked, she'd sat in her purloined apartment drawing diagrams of the humans walking around outside. The glorious firsts, blithely unaware they'd been chosen.

Out of two pale people, the lightest. Out of two of medium height, the shortest. Out of two fat ones, the thinnest. Out of two quiet ones, the loudest. Out of a dealer and a man behind the wheel waiting to score coke, the man. Her notebook was awash with combustible pairs, stick figures rushing off the page, begging for a second chance before darkness overtook them.

Rain pissed onto the streets outside the café, humid, *wanderlusting*, munched up a split second later by the boiling blue skies that always erupted in the aftermath. The face had been talking to her. It had seen the first lunar landing, the countdown to the H-bomb dropping on Hiroshima, the first lanes of the interstate highway being built atop gutted neighborhoods. Fluttering moments pressed between the pages of textbooks, frozen in amber fever dreams regurgitated on eleventh-grade history tests. Every chair she sat in, or table she put her shit down on, had a memory jockeying for her attention. She closed her eyes and searched for a command post, a warm brain bed to sleep in to preserve for eternity.

After her first operation, the invading memories exploded. Descending on her as the anesthesia wore off, sensing she would be a proper, obedient host. A field mouse in retreat. She'd looked in the mirror and a void stared back at her. Eyes, nose, and mouth dissolving into a fire lake, a welter of Halloween yellows, oranges, and reds; then the clang of a school bell in an ice storm, airplane toilets flushing in unison ten seconds before a catastrophic engine failure, a jail cell door thudding closed. The only way she could stop the memories of the others from coming was through the game. Plucking random people from the street, mini marts, laundromats, bus stops, post offices, cars speeding past her in traffic. Drawing Noah's Ark twos on her arms. Plugging in a formula to stem the gargantuan tide of all the humans who had ever crossed her path and the ones who hadn't yet. The living and the dead bearing down on her with saber-toothed tiger teeth.

First, the memory motherfuckers had gotten her fired from a hoagie sandwich shop. Then ousted from a temp gig filing car insurance claims. Then cut loose from a weekend pittance doing seasonal fruit cup demos in a supermarket, a dash of luck because the store had burned to the ground a week later. The produce flame broiled right before the checkers' eyes.

What was the advantage of a magical power if it didn't do good shit for you? If it didn't hoist you into the stratosphere, into the pantheon of fake gods, plunk you down into the swampland promise of eternity that every human who'd ever lived buck danced for, clamored for, wanted to kill for. Magic was cheap. Prophecies were cheap. Spirits were parasitic, puffs of swirling ash. Clouds burst up by a jet plane. Cold fact was, in the black of night, waiting for her alarm to go off again, she had no one to confess to but the dead: restless and sitting in judgment, jesters ping-ponging between the four walls of her head as she dressed to go to work.

She had always wanted to travel the world. But not like this. Not jerking awake every other minute, feverish with the gurgle of sunsetting voices.

"Closing in fifteen minutes," the barista yelled from behind the counter.

The subway station was a block away. She could ride the trains until they shut down at 2 a.m., burrow underneath a baseball cap, disguise herself as a white man, a replica of her father; anonymous, shape-shifting in Twinkie paste mellow yellow, eluding the storm troopers who swarmed through the open turnstiles, hot for fresh meat.

"Fifteen minutes," the barista said again to a trickle of new customers. Students from the beauty college tumbled in, stooping over from rinsing out dye jobs all day, lusting to cut a caffeine trail through the grunge of hunger and fatigue slick upon them like an afterbirth. A totem pole with stringy twigs on his head slapped three dollars onto the counter, and she could feel him, a skittering soul on ice, gnashing at the remnants of tattletales who'd spat and shat on him for sporting pink nail polish at five years old in a Catholic school coatroom crusty with soiled nun's habits. What was the dividing line between her and him? Between them and her. What rogue gene hum determined the artificiality of separate brains and limbs and nervous systems in the junkyard of humans?

She watched them slurp and carouse, grouping them again into pairs, calculating who'd go aboard, who'd be left behind, who'd be swallowed up in the cyclone gathering on the horizon, the plague waiting to devour the iniquitous. The barista called out again. Fourteen minutes, thirteen, twelve. Eleven. Channeling the same hospital delivery room voice that kicked Briony out of the womb and into the boiling light and heat, into the death sentence of passing days.

The barista clattered over to her table with the trash bag for a final sweep, scooping up napkins and the cup with her name on it. Briony watched the glowing faces arrayed around the store, fools united in anticipation of the young night unfurling ahead. Deliciously numb. She chuckled to herself as the windows rattled. Car alarms ripped through the air. Beetle drops of rain plunked onto the sidewalk. The sky's mouth opened over the waiting paper ark.

The barista came up behind her. She took off her glasses and squinted at the sketchpad. Briony turned. Up close, she saw incision lines zigzagging around her cheekbones, tiny spider stitches sewn where the boundaries of her former face ended and a transplant began.

Briony recoiled and squinted back.

"Nice drawing. You've got a lot of talent, *Briony*," the barista said, sounding out each syllable of her name as she read it from the cup. "Funny thing about humans. The best have long memories. The worst are amnesiacs. Every single one gets hung up, putting shit into categories."

She picked up the sketchpad, traced her finger on the ark, the wind whipping, beginning a soft howl. "So maybe you and I can walk the gangplank together, huh? And, by the way, you're first."

L&D

WHAT WOULD HAVE BEEN MY life is blackness. But here I am, on my skateboard. *Kick, ride, kick.* Black as the rhythm of stones being thrown against a car bumper or respirators sighing in unison, marking time in intensive care. It is me against traffic. Faceless boy. Nameless face. A stick figure watching the preeners lolling toothily into their car side mirrors, the press-on nail tex- ters smearing out the seconds between red light, green light; the dandelion yellow school buses idling out the last twenty minutes before the school bell rings and a blitzkrieg of jeering children descend.

The first time I heard boys laughing, they were playing the dozens about punk-faced "fags." The punk in B6 who walked like a princess. The punk in the cafeteria who spoke all proper and shit. The punk who brought a lunchbox with the daintiest, fair- iest of pink in the logo. Batted his eyes. Undressed us with each blink as we stormed the urinals in the bathroom. Pirouetted and spread his arms out wide, lissome as Bambi. I was ready to join the punk conspiracy, to surrender to them, waiting outside the gates of the playground with a pack of Red Vines for anyone who'd let me in. I could read their lips against the thrum of the dodge ball, feel the savage smash of rubber on the asses of stragglers caught in the fifth graders' gladiator pen. I willed myself into the middle of each game, snatching the ball from a third-grade piglet, tongue green with jawbreakers from trick-or-treat.

The tall one with the Hello Kitty keychain has been my nurse for the past few days. From 6 a.m. to 6 p.m., we're united in smell: arthritis cream under her fingernails, tomato juice on her breath filching into my sweaty white hospital sheets as she soldiers through her routine noting each new arrival—the hushed parade of doleful relatives, the mothers doped up, zombified, bereft after the furor of delivery.

Every misshapen infant skull is part of her queenly dominion. She measures and sizes up and scrapes off dead skin, the room a blur of lumpy, wriggling, pustulous bodies. And when no one is looking, she takes my foot into her hands. Sucks each toe clean as a finger-licking wishbone while snow piles up all around us in plastic drifts. As a child in Minnesota, snow season was her most treasured memory. The glee of pushing her baby brothers on their sled, plying them with snowballs, a blow to the head for each sin they'd committed by seven, an ice bomb to the occipital for being dirty blond little princes to her mousy brown drudge.

All my dodge ball boys get hot and heavy for the tease of snow. Dream of pummeling each other into snowy oblivion, of coming out French kissing, cub tits hardening beneath their Laker jerseys. In the Southern California drear, the endless bleak of newborn June, none of them have seen snow. But I have, and now I will be their secret envy. I will be picked first, allowed to cut in line, to have my pick of ice cream, to get dibs on the biggest scoop with chocolate sprinkles. I'll send my drippy valentine to the nurse as she suctions fluid from my belly button, readjusts the tubes taped to my nose, diddles the gilt K-mart cross in her pocket, gives me her God's blessing in a gin-soaked whisper. She's been hitting it, hitting it all night in her studio apartment over the twenty-four-hour Laundromat on Berendo. Hitting it as the talk shows and sitcom reruns bled into vibrator infomercials. Hitting it as the test pattern prattle of the morning news crested and she spray starched her uniform into the ironing board, annihilating every crease and line so it would pass management's daily inspection. Our Lord, art thou in heaven, betrayer of little children, hallowed be thy name, giving no quarter to their innocence rolling right out the womb, content to be MIA as we all burn.

The NICU nurses taped a name to my bed. First name, last name, guttural letters in Martian code. When I tried to pronounce it, all I got was a glob of old amniotic fluid, underwater spit the nurse dabbed quickly from my mouth.

A boy on the playground has the same name. Initials are NK. His mother comes to pick him up after school. I slide into the backseat with my Red Vines and my Ruff and Tuff lunchbox, nod brightly to his boasts about winning the candy drive and acing the new video games his friend Antoine lent him, wondering if he'll notice me after all these weeks of obedience. In school, he is tender, wriggling meat on the spit of the big girls prowling the lower-grade playground for water balloon virgins to bounce them off of. Because his ride comes every day like clockwork, he's the mama's boy, her double, her twin; *look, they have the same squint when they shit.* Sitting here, I see the symmetry in the backs of their heads. His picks up where hers left off. He is her when she got knocked off her tricycle, stole jawbreakers from the corner store, darted out into the middle of rush-hour traffic on a triple dare, bit the hand of the nice family man with the gray-blue eyes who jerked off in the ashtray of his car and tried to grab her when the lunch bell rang. The crumbs of her DNA make a horseshoe birthmark on the side of his neck, crackling through each dark tendril of hair, bequeathing the code that will make his hairline recede in ten years at the height of his prancing *studliness.*

We watch the kids swarm the 7-11 with fistfuls of quarters for Hot Cheetos, aisles ablaze with Friday afternoon emancipation. They hoist Cheeto bags over their heads like a big game, brushing by the church boy predators tricked out in Jesus bling, looking for someone to mate with. I lean into N's ear. His right

35

lobe is all baby oil and pea soup and the musty smooch of the family Cocker Spaniel. We roll through the numbered streets to his house, past the dead stillness of men clustered on porches in jobless midday communion. Past the check cashing places, the body shops, the blinding kindergarten bliss of the crowded public pool. He'll invite me up to his room to watch cartoons, be my hope to die, my refuge for one full episode. *I'd go anywhere with you*, I croak, blowing dandruff from his bony shoulders.

Last night, I took a crap for the first time. A visiting team of specialists, *neonatologists*, they called them, clucked over it and proclaimed it a good sign. They jotted the miracle down on their clipboards as they made the rounds through our gurgling colony of in-limbo infants, secretly swapping bets on who'd make it out alive to taste the wild blue, to see the sunshine unfiltered by the grates of hospital windows, to revel in the stench of their first fuck, feel the highway slithering under them on a cross-country drive taking the wheel with a newly minted license. To grow old enough to fear death and start the fool's bargain for more time.

You're a perfect angel, the nurse whispered to me tonight. She ran down her checklist again, radiant it was the end of her shift, avoiding the downward sag of my shriveled testicles, my purple lips puckering full tilt, listening for the balloon's hiss of late-night traffic trickling to the south, the north, chasing infinity. The world becoming a car, revving on a twenty-four-hour loop, ornery as I flatline toward it on my skateboard. *Kick, ride, kick.*

10:20

COME HELL OR HIGH WATER, he was gonna be sharp for his first day of work as a rent-a-cop at the bling, bling palace on Fig and 8ᵗʰ.

Hector stood in the library bathroom mirror, counting the wrinkles tic-tac-toeing from his temple to his right eye. He'd noticed them five years ago, covering them with his hair, grown out longer since he'd been kicked out of the Corps. The right side had always been his coyote side, the wily side, the one he could lie out of and escape detection most times. The side guaranteed to throw interlopers off the scent. The side kissed to pieces by his last fair-weather love. The side zapped first by the laser light of the new world the morning he was born, the countdown to death beginning in a black whimper.

Forty-five and between lovers was when the wrinkles started multiplying like gremlins. Bursting from temple to eye in a mushroom cloud, peeking out contrarily from the well-placed lock of wavy hair he wore cascading from the top of his head in confetti strands. He was the darkest one in his family, but his skin ratted out his age like a saggy, baggy Caucasian. No cosmic justice. No quarter. He looked at himself in store windows and thought, *What the fuck happened to Black don't crack?* Wondered who this traitor was. *Who was this muskrat who'd choked in the heat of a court-martial hearing on a cloudless spring day?*

Ten o'clock, and he had to be quick. Dodge the devil hour of bad luck. Put his uniform on, shave, comb his hair, brush his

Sikivu Hutchinson

teeth, do an underarm wash before the bathroom was taken hostage by a boatload of pungent men pinching in their ass cheeks from holding it for hours. This lot, a prim minority too persnickety to do it in the street or join the hunt for Porta-Potties downtown.

Ever since he'd gotten evicted from his motel room, he'd fallen into the rhythm. When the library opened in the morning, the men staked out the bathrooms on each floor. A few settled down in the stalls with a magazine from the stacks for an extended crap session. The head librarian got wind of it and created a bathroom patrol, unleashing a detail of janitors every hour on the hour to do a purge.

The first day of work, and he was late, dragging on four hours of sleep punctured by a recurring dream of walking through a zoo with empty animal cages. It's broad daylight, and the blur of a crowd in the distance gathered around the last cage. Men in fedoras with their backs to him. Jostling, elbowing, pointing silently at the inmate inside. The closer he got, he saw the *men* were a regiment of mega-rats with greasy whiskers. Jostling, pointing, pressing hungrily into the bars of the cage, the air filling with the whoosh of whipping tails. Damp and hollow, fading into a jump cut of his court-martial hearing.

The judge asked him to stand. His knees buckled. Piss streamed down his bum right leg. The jury panel laughed as the cocker spaniel foreman fished through his body, pulling out boomerangs, ropes, baseballs. Props from his childhood to bury him. To stuff his torso into freshly dug earth beneath the courtroom. A gallery of talcum powder white faces stared down at him. Grunts with their limbs blasted off. Vietnam generals puffing their chests out, bursting with prisoner of war bone medals.

Was it a dream or real that they had called Minnesota in to testify? Two hours into the proceedings, at 10:00 a.m., he walked an invisible tightrope from his chair to the stand, his gaze a uni-

38

verse away from Hector. All the white boy military attorneys had coached him not to tread like a pussy. *Be the Indian brave you are, not that predator's bitch,* they gossiped about in mess hall. The official storyline was that Hector had taken advantage of Minnesota's small-town kindness, his gentleness, his naivete. The official line on the transcripts that would be stored in his file in a vault for one hundred years was that he had jumped him, bent his will, turned him into a convert the almighty couldn't redeem.

The night before the hearing, Hector had stayed up, pacing, holding his old grade school crucifix so tightly it cut a bloody moat into his palm, the worthless thing dusty with disuse. *Don't ges-tic-u-late, don't slur, keep your head at a ninety-degree angle,* they'd growled. If you want us to save your shiftless ass from jail and stay in the Corps, boy, you better know how to perform.

It had been some other man's life, not his. A shadow he'd picked apart, his hands coming up empty, paralyzed. After he'd been discharged, and his military benefits dried up, he'd wandered the city. Couches, shelters, train stations, freeway underpasses, abandoned cars, libraries, twenty-four-hour supermarkets gleaming with forbidden fruit. Selling blowjobs for a few nights indoors to have his own bed, sink, toilet, fifty square foot space to think, until he was back on the edge of a cliff, staring down at bottom.

He squeezed soap from the dispenser into his palm, rubbed it into his right cheek, smoothed the bags under his eyes, the black patch of rogue chin stubble. He wet his razor and shaved, listening to a commotion beginning behind the stalls. It was the jury again. At 10:19 a.m., tapping their feet in unison, building to a slow march, excavating the dump he took for clues of his deviance. Who was this phantom in the mirror, blinking back at him, a gumbo of spider veins and blisters and moles mocking his four-and-a-half decades? He turned, and the marching stopped. The foreman's voice sang out.

Minnesota's testimony played as nine minutes of not looking at Hector. A blizzard of yessirs, nosirs, his bottomless eyes taped to the prosecutor's Wingtip shoes as he lied about what Hector had done to him, tall tales smooth as buttercream on hot fingertips, down to niggling little details about positions and orifices. Hector couldn't say he blamed Minnesota for lying to try and save himself. He'd heard that Blacks got the most expulsions for being queer, or perceived that way. Ejected as so-called blue discharges starting back in the twenties. Waking up to the shitstorm of being branded inverts, undesirable, the stench following them to the grave.

The marching in the bathroom stalls started up again. Ripped a hole in the floor to the beat of taps. He was gonna be sharp for his first day. Show them what an ex-Trig whiz could do. Move up the ranks and be running the place in a year. *Find Minnesota, fuck him, then beat his brains in.* This was the time traitor speaking to him in the mirror. The side that would brook no forgiveness.

Standing there, clean-shaven, ready for the brave new world at last, he could taste the memory of that Saturday when he first saw him. Minnesota had been trying to balance his hat and his legal books with one hand, eating an orange with the other, pieces of peel lacquered to his lips. The Virginia sky was coughing up flurries, dappling his corkscrew curls, the only inheritance he knew from his mother, dead at childbirth at twenty-two.

Some of the men had gotten leave time off base. The land-locked ones kept the place humming, playing poker and video games and dominos; knocking back 40s; ribbing Minnesota, the perfectionist. *M-dog always with a book. M-dog blabbing about his legal exit plan strategy to anyone within earshot; the goody-two-shoes who'd dedicate his life to doing pro bono for the downtrodden, the penniless, the hard up. M-law-and-order, doggy style.*

Hector hated games, was shitty at competition, so he watched the others, listened to Hank Williams twang in desperation on his Walkman, tapping out "I'm So Lonesome I Could Cry" in three-quarters time. He'd seen Minnesota in the dining hall sitting alone, sinking under daydream waves as he scanned his law books. He hadn't looked at him. Made a point to stare past him, to the dreamy blue miniature screen of a space invader game blasting asteroids into digital infinity and his roommate maneuvering a joy stick with his left hand, freshly bandaged from smashing his girlfriend's bedroom wall. Macho man lit with booze and bud and fear that his weak little, throbbing little, knock-kneed little heart would be hunted down, cracked open, and read by the drill sergeant. So many of them are like that. Shark boys, barrio boys, fugitive rednecks from teeming cities and pinprick towns, itching for a war or an ambush to tear them down and Humpty-Dumpty them back together again as brave, fearless commandos.

Busy not looking at Minnesota, Hector noticed how tall he stood. Palm tree lean. The dark, *lickable* set of his shoulders, the same untouchable cool as the shark boys, a voice like rainwater pounding on a metal roof. If he got a taste of him, got to take him in his arms and rock him to the end of time. If. If. If. To hell with the fucking one-night stands. With all the panting, clawing possession, the trifling games of will-he-or-won't-he call and close the deal. If he got him, it would be crazy love or bust, the tea leaves of their surrender blaring in megaphone.

Before him, there had only been one other boy. A bonehead who had mangled Hector's name from the back of the bus after he had dropped his baseball cap. Bonehead had picked it up, read the initials Hector's mother had embroidered in gold thread on the brim, and put it on as a joke, following him off the bus to the bowling alley where the neighborhood kids played pinball.

"Whaddaya want, man?" he asked, voice cracking. He would fight if he had to. Bonehead was shorter than him but bulldog stocky, pants slipping and sliding in a homeboy sag, golden arch eyebrows betraying every dastardly inner thought, flower petal mouth drooping with sadness.

"This hat is the shit," bonehead said, flipping up the brim. "Where'd you get it, and how much?"

The bonehead collected caps. Everywhere he went, he picked up one. Liquor stores, Goodwills, grandma's house, dumpsters, classrooms. His stock was junk to primo. They stood in front of the bowling alley, sizing each other up until the bonehead challenged him to pinball. If the bonehead lost, he'd cough up twenty bucks and the cap. If Hector lost, Bonehead would keep the cap.

"Win-win for you, chief," he said as they went inside.

Bronco Billy. Demolition Derby. Bombs Away. The pinball lights dazzled, set the alley on fire. They decided on a World War II game. Downing battleships in the Pacific until the bonehead ran out of quarters, his fingers crusted over with motor oil and grape juice. Bonehead's name was Roman. He spent the first few games shit talking Hector with his pell-mell Spanglish and tall tales about how he was going to blow up bigger than Jesus one day and ditch the neighborhood, charter a Learjet with money from a top-secret invention.

"Everyone in the world wants to turn back the clock and do their lives over again," he said. "You figure out a way to pop a pill or shoot up or hotwire people's pea fucking brains, you'd make a gazillion. You figure that out and every peon up in here would want to suck me clean as old fishbones."

He said this eating French fries from the snack bar, mashing them in his mouth three at a time. He grinned at Hector through gleaming gold teeth after having beat him at every game, stoked about winning the baseball cap "fair and square." His teeth gleamed so brightly Hector was hypnotized, seeing tiny little men surfing the waves in each molar. He'd wanted to believe Roman so badly. Wanted him to turn into the avenger he fantasized about when he was getting beaten by his stepfather. Into the psycho rider who would descend on cue, trampling homeboy on a beautiful black horse, banishing him to a bottomless hell he half-believed was fake anyway. Thinking maybe some of the magic would rub off, wormhole him out of the ramshackle triplex apartment building he shared with three generations of relatives across the street from an incinerator.

Roman said he was twenty-five, but his expired driver's license ratted him out as thirty. The farthest he'd ever gone was boot camp, two years in the Corps, dishonorably discharged for passing bad checks. Hector started hanging out at the bowling alley waiting for him. There were eyes everywhere, clocking, charting his and Roman's every move. The cherry Slurpee fiend shoe checker watching them make their rounds of the pinball machines. The lifers just off work, settling into marathon beer-soaked games. The manager manically sweeping up after every spill and goo stain on the floors, overcharging them for onion rings, ogling Hector's ass through tinted brown horn-rims. Roman had racked up the highest score on Bombs Away. A legend now, with his name in lights. A hero dodging shrapnel over a cartoon Pearl Harbor. A slayer smacking down bullnecked Nazis. And when they kissed for the third time behind the bus stop, bending around the stink spawn of the incinerator, double-checking to make sure there were no dagger eyes, Hector's heart did taps against his will.

The killers came on the one day Hector missed going to the bowling alley because he had to babysit his little cousins. Three runty white boys waited for Roman outside, sloshing around in the first driving rain of April. Shadowing him with Kool-Aid grins as the water swirled and roared on the soon-to-be repo'ed beaters in the parking lot. A tournament going on all week. Five-thousand-dollar grand prize from a Masonic temple. The pride of East L.A. versus Omaha. Reports were, at first, that they'd shipped in from Nebraska with the rest of the grizzled herd, coked up and hot for revenge after East L.A. mopped the floor with them. But, nah, *they were a different kind of homegrown white boy*, a witness on a dirt bike deadpanned into the news cameras.

SIKIVU HUTCHINSON

Hector found out about the murder while channel surfing later that night, the little cousins snoring at his elbow, angel faces splattered with the vanilla pudding he gave them for dinner. Just as he was about to turn off the TV, he saw an aerial view of the bowling alley, the blond anchor lady on KTTV reading in her rat-a-tat-tat voice about a punk hood stomped down to the guts for stealing a diamond ring from a pawn shop for his fiancée.

On the RTD bus the next morning, all the regulars could talk about in the back was that bonehead Roman who up and got himself killed. Cackling and shaking their heads as Hector turned his head to the window, to the sky, to the magic carpet clouds beckoning with evaporating white fingers.

When military recruiters dive-bombed his school looking for enlistees, he thought running away so far no one would ever be able to find him would be the cure for the pissing emptiness in his heart. To see the same slice of the world the bonehead had seen at twenty. Walk the same path, escape his fate of never amounting to anything. The first time he flew in a plane coming home from the base, he looked for Roman among the cumulonimbus. Dreamed of punching through the window, reunited, sucked up into the wild blue. He steeled himself against the turbulence, biting his lip, secretly kneading new galaxies into his armrest so no one could see him going bat shit with fear as the DC-10 jet whipped back and forth.

The grind of boot camp took his mind off Roman. A battering ram of sit-ups, push-ups, jumping jacks, obstacle courses, mud runs; all the while, the drill sergeant was calling his squadron shitwad, monkey motherfuckers; blowing his body up with an interstellar fatigue that had him reciting the alphabet backward to stay conscious. After two years, he'd whittled down to a fighting weight of 160. Then Desert Storm broke out, and all the grunts were on edge about being sent up, coming back as Kibbles 'n Bits. Rumor was, the darker you were, the more likely it would

44

go down. The poorer you were, the more the pine box would be waiting. Saturday nights, bored, scared, antsy, backstroking in the warm Carolina rain, the boys in his barracks would take turns doing target practice, peeing on a poster of Saddam Hussein dolled up in fishnets and red Dorothy in Oz heels. Whoever sprays crooked is a Nancy boy. Whoever misses the mark more than twice is a eunuch. Whoever misses three times will be the first to get shipped out. Whoever can catch a bullet in their teeth can stop time. "Whoever, whoever, whoever," they chanted in unison, taming the unknown, prying it apart as they drifted off, the weekend crashing and burning at their feet.

The morning he noticed the new boy from Minnesota was the morning after he'd dreamed he was in a pinball game, being punted around between ace fighter jets, pink plasticene breasts, the neon six-packs of G. I. Joes; fighting for his life until Roman plucked him out, whispering sweet nothings into his crying eyes. Tall drink of water Minnesota had a lemon twist smile, a bullet arm, a steel trap brain, and a passion for legal books. Star quarterback in a two-horse, white, hayseed town that loved his dirty drawers with a cherry on top until his throw went sideways. Then he was just another unemployed brown buck, fucking up the census numbers.

"Underneath it all, they're the terrorists, the real ones," he said, pointing to his sliver of the universe on the mess hall map of the U.S. The hordes that slept, ate, and shat football, parading him around when he scored, vultures picking over his flesh after the orgy glow of the season faded. "The corps was the same," he said. "Same playbook, different armpits in time." He'd enlisted because of the drumbeat from his mother, aunties, and uncles, a chorus busting out in his ear at Christmas dinner, drunk on tales of martyred Korean War grandfathers who'd drowned in enemy blood.

Once he'd made the decision to go, it gave momentum to the wasted days of sending out applications for data processing jobs that went unanswered, while the white kids who'd flunked out of business college got hired for middle management. "Same play-book, different galaxy," he ranted. The sergeants warning him to shut up about the U.S., trashing the Middle East around the commanders. It was what Hector loved and feared about him, watching him make the tobacco spitters squirm, admiring his pluck and sass, wondering if even a quarter of it could rub off on him, help him come up with a plan to quiet the locomotive rattle of emptiness in his head. Minnesota was Roman but smoother, wiser, a delectable gleam to his teeth, bucked from thumb sucking, huddled with a security blanket in the electrical storms that cracked his hometown in two. Minnesota was the first one he'd met in the corps who didn't hide his sweetness, his wanderlust, his feline curiosity in a vise grip, squeezing punk tears out of his victims. He'd taken care of his little cousins, same as Hector. Watched them do burp contests and fight sleep and stick gum in each other's hair for sport.

"Were we ever that age?" he whispered to Hector one night, the two of them intertwined under a fistful of stars. They traced phantom constellations on each other's lips, comparing the exact coordinates of the portals they'd fantasized escaping into when they were being beaten for talking back or looking sideways at their daddies. "The only way I survived," he said, kissing Minnesota's earlobes down to the wax, "was to pretend I could teleport the fuck out of there anytime I wanted."

Pretending. A superhero cape flapping behind his back as he jumped from his bunk bed onto the pretend lava boiling on the rug. Pretending, in spindly high heels, orange smeared lipstick, black spider lashes he'd watched his tía put on reluctantly, egged on by her sisters, even though she wasn't trying to catch no man. Pretending, he was a real *machista* at thirteen, falling in line, lockstep with the catcalling Catholic school boys lapping up girls' fear as they heckled them on the streets.

He was drifting the summer before deployment when he pretended Minnesota was Roman, and the rumors about them started out as graffiti in the bathroom stalls. A penis rising from a stick figure bent over like a dog with their initials on it. Nursery rhyme taunts chanted after lights-out under the hiss of mutant mosquitos. Fee-fi-fo-fum. Be nimble, be quick. Huff and puff and blow it all down.

Who was this wraith staring back at him in the mirror? This haunted house of a man willing the clock hands to sleep? If he could close his eyes, snap his fingers, live in the sweet cream of stopped time. Peel Minnesota's betrayal away from his memory.

Instead, it was 10:15 a.m., and his new boss would have to wait a bit more. Wait for him to spray cologne on his neck, scrape the last pinch of toothpaste from the tube, finger wash his teeth to a yellow gleam, suck his gut in, ease into the old 6:00 a.m. boots-on-the-ground formation drill. *Promised you*, he thought, *it'd be worth the wait*, 'cause now he looked semi-presentable. Wouldn't be confused for one of the 10:20 a.m. bathroom grifters funking up the library stacks from geology to romance.

"Nothing happened," he had told his defense counsel, the clammy-handed, tripe-breathed, ten-times-trying-to-pass-the-bar lawyer the corps had appointed to him when his grandmother couldn't raise enough money to hire a private attorney. "Nothing happened," he told him once, twice, three times, shitting bricks as he sat in the grim-walled deposition room where the second half of his life passed before his eyes. After Minnesota had screwed him, his throat went to rust as he tried not to watch the clock and imagine all the men who'd come before him marooned there, waiting for the vise to tighten around their necks.

"Nothing from nothing," he had said, suppressing a laugh as he raised his right hand to take the oath on the stand. Was he free to lie if he didn't believe the Bible? Could he press the button down on the big black recorder by the court reporter and stop everything? Teleport back to the bowling alley and the damp toadstool smell of Roman's sweatshirt gagging him as he came?

47

It was 10:19 a.m., and the rumblings began on the south side of the library. The pitter-patter of big feet in the corridor of the astrophysics section, advancing armies, frantic threesomes, stooges following close on each other's heels, faces flushed with ecclesiastic relief as they claimed their bathroom stalls, latched the doors, squatted, grunted in unison. Hector turned on the faucets to drown out the thud of each load. He shoved his stuff in his bag and listened for the descent of the library stack monitors, a field of crickets twittering in midnight slick.

Almost ready now. The right and left sides of his face in league with each other, his posture correct, his shirt not yet drooping with midmorning sweat. Feeling now, that he could face the seconds, minutes, hours of the new workday head-on, not another rent-a-cop elbowing through the sprawl of a county payday line, but an attaché, an intel gatherer on a top-secret mission.

The middle stall door swung open. He squinted. In the mirror, he saw the jury foreman zipping his pants as he hobbled out. They locked eyes. Then, the man looked down, fishing in his pocket. He unfolded a cap onto the wet sink.

"Where you off to?" he asked.

"Work."

"You know what they say about idle hands."

"Nah, I don't."

"They're the devil's playground."

He smoothed out the cap and put it on Hector's head, the gold threading of his initials glinting in the dingy bathroom light. "Won this in a pinball game from some dumb shit a few years back. Maybe it'll be your good luck charm today."

Big Death

A THOUSAND WARHEADS RAIN DOWN on the Walmart parking lots. Big fat promise rings pelt Modesto, Orange, L.A., Riverside. Sleek, built-for-speed bodies manned by Slim Pickens delirious in a buckaroo bloat, his sweet new spurs digging into the letters *d-a-n-g-e-r* tattooed on the airframe. A quarter note before nuclear winter, and there is a run on Super Sippers and beef ramen noodles at the strip malls. There's a frenzy synchronized clear across five counties, mastodon fathers shoving econo boxes of Frosted Flakes into their baskets. Chain-smoking mothers sweating out their purple eye shadow in the fifteen items only line, loading eighteen onto the belt. It's almost noon, Americana feedbag hour, and Riley is being pushed by her mother in a shopping cart. She is way too big and too old to fit in it; she is fifty years old, in fact, her feet scraping the ground in that unseemly, trifling way that her mother always dragged her about. Stand up straight, suck your stomach in, unroll those eyes, and walk like a young lady, not a stevedore. Her mother is whirling-dervish thin, handy with endearments, a whisperer with tectonic moods. She had a God-given talent for losing their station wagon in big box parking lots.

They have been looking for the car for what seems like hours. Riley is hot and sweaty and hungry, swimming in an ill-fitting training bra. A security guard bobbing and weaving to the song "Atomic Dog" watches them hunt for it in the shimmering sea of overheated beaters. She fans herself with a coupon clipper, busting out, "Why must I feel like that? Why must I chase the cat?" as toddlers swarm the painted hobby horse ride at the exit door, brawling over who was first in line.

Riley fends off the drivers hovering behind them for a space with her new baby blue sun visor as the last bomb falls. She flicks the butt end of the warhead into the windshield of a burgundy Pacer nosing into the wheels of the shopping cart, and waits as the car explodes in a million lug nuts. She shrugs. Could have stayed at home and had the whole house to herself while both of her parents were out on the prowl for lunch meat at the grocery store. She could have staked out a whole section of the den for new masturbation scenes in front of the TV, but she was lured, finally, by the promise of watermelon bubble gum with green stripes. She and her sort of junior high school best friend Kat were supposed to meet in the parking lot, but Kat had stood her up for Hula-Hooping with another girl, tired of the dull as dirt afternoons they'd spent lying in wait outside the grocery store for the gumball machine man to load a new flavor into the machine. They'd flitted around each other in a steam of trash talk, nickel-and-dime bets, speculation, monologues, making moon eyes at gumball man's skinny, quivering frame.

When they saw the bright green globes of gum gleaming behind the glass, they were already stuffing them between their jaws for a bubble blowing smackdown mentally. Kat is bad, but Riley is badder, faster, her technique honed to perfection to chew out all the sugar before launching the bubble into the zone. She blows a goiter sized nugget, then watches Kat try to top it with an abortive sputter. She snickers and struts and reboots, chicle breaching her blood-brain barrier as she makes a triple bubble, big enough to wrap around the warhead and send in a valentine sling to all the Mayberry RFDs.

On weekends, Riley got lost in a dream derby. Sleep. Delicious, hallowed, sleep. Trying to go back to sleep again. Trying to recreate the exact preliminary stupor of falling into nothingness, her spinal cord going slack with reverie as she flopped down in the bed in the same position, breathing through her nose, hapless after fifteen minutes of listening to the gleeful drill of the dental hygienist next door. In the daytime, the building is home to a dentist, a CPA, and a proctologist—a trio of waxy nosed white men hatched from the Valley, all prodding and pressing on the other side of her bedroom wall. From late morning to late afternoon, the wall hums with new findings. Patients enter and exit discreetly, slithering into the waiting room with expressions of pinched insouciance, the Muzak speaker pumping them rich with aural cyanide. When she is not working, she becomes an excavator of the hairy butt cheeks of middle-aged Anglo-Saxons. Her fantasy, her life's dream, is to spelunk all the wayward twists and turns of evolution seared into the dimples on their asses. A pockmark here, a crater there, vestiges of genetic roads not taken.

Lately, her dreams have been wall-to-wall Kat. She had a habit of calling Riley collect from payphones or showing up at her laundromat, asking for money. Kat had worked fast-food jobs all up and down Interstate 5, breaking the streak when she got a job at a pool cue factory. She was cleaning bathrooms one afternoon when a water main exploded in the men's. Water blasted through the stalls, sending her swimming on her back to the parking lot with a pair of cracked vertebrae. A week later, the company went bankrupt, stiffing her with emergency room healthcare coverage and a pocketful of homeopathic pills. Riley hadn't wanted to see her laid up, delirious, raving, milking it for sympathy and more dough to piss away on who knew the fuck what. To Riley, hospitals were a plague. A smelly shitty paperwork maze no one escaped from. After weighing pros and cons over bags of Doritos, she went to see Kat grudgingly. She snatched some wilted flowers from a vase in one of the waiting rooms, steeling herself for a spectacle. Kat was asleep when she went in. Floating in a corona

51

of blood flecked white sheets, mouth twitching in debate. The nurses said she would wake up, but she stayed asleep, or pretended to. Riley left the flowers on her nightstand and crept out; past the empty visitors' register, past the terminal patients in the next ward baying at the moon for a swift end.

After Kat was discharged, she got a room in a downtown hotel, living in her car when the landlady evicted her for falling behind on rent. She stopped calling Riley collect, stopped showing up at the laundry, stopped paying on the PO Box she'd had for ten years. Hit churches for the food pantries, claiming she had kids so she could get more food. Saying God owed her anyway for being a deadbeat in the wilderness when she was molested by a predator pastor whose wife groomed girls for him in her spick and span baby blue Coupe de Ville.

At 5 a.m. every morning, she left snickering messages on Riley's answering machine. *Wake up, fathead. It's time to go to work. Turn that fucking TV off—it's propaganda. Get the remote, and turn that shit off right now. I know you had it on all night.*

Riley liked commercials with the sound turned off. Liked to watch the shame of Americana on parade, luxuriated in all the waste and buying orgy banality, the bleak heart of whiteness oozing like filling from a big fat éclair with every super-size drink, weed whacker, or leather fanny pack in heavy rotation. She had become one of those people who turn on the TV as soon as they come home from work, rationalizing she was doing it to drown out the bleed of traffic noise from outside. Rationalizing it was some under-the-radar political project, a species study for survival after the biblical flood that would wash away all the bacon-double-cheeseburger-eating sinners from under her window.

She would be among the few spared when the onslaught began. Silver surfing a great white wave that would snatch up houses and cars and mailboxes and streetlights like so much Play-Doh. At the end of one night, when she'd put her dentures in the bathroom to soak and checked the lock on the front door one last time, she settled down in her ten-speed recliner to watch the eleven o'clock news. The newscaster's mug gave way to an image of Kat being led away in handcuffs with her head down. She was suspected of planting razor blades in Halloween candy. Chocolate cherry chews and a candy bar scarfed down by three white kids playing near her parked car in a lot in Hermosa. The kids had been rushed to emergency, had their stomachs pumped twice, then been prayed over in 'round the clock vigils by the local parish church. Their parents clutched each other and railed to the cameras with vengeful, bloodshot eyes, knowing the world was watching for the fate of the would-be killer.

Riley spent the rest of that night clicking around for news reports, each flash of Kat perp walking sending a ripple of nausea and excitement through her. They'd picked her up a block from the beach, sitting in her car, smoking pot, and blasting metal on an old Walkman. She'd always been partial to eighties hair bands with pockmarked skin, the windmill guitar solos that screamed into the ether, the arena rock crowds sucking down their testosterone like fruit punch. She burrowed into fret boards and lived there, a permanent dog whistle ring in her ears from a jillion hours of intergalactic flight. When the two black and whites pulled up next to Kat, they'd confiscated a Malibu Barbie from her, cuffed her, and taken her to the women's jail downtown, unarmed and dangerous and speaking in some savage tongue.

The paper delivery people planted her picture on front lawns across the city, the perp walk melting in the morning dew and sprinkler runoff. A fifty-four-year-old Negress wielding a dirty Barbie over her head. The shot had been taken in color, a florid medley of golds and greens that made her skin look darker.

When she got to work the next morning, Riley took the paper from the staff breakroom and hid it in her cubicle. A few bystanders in the picture stood on the margins, gawking from plastic coffee cups, cheeks flushed with righteous indignation.

The pixels that made up Kat's face began to melt into goo the longer she looked at them. Her sunken eyes lit up like poker chips behind the tinted bifocals she'd had since tenth grade. That afternoon, she caught fragments of conversation about Kat and the crime in the tenth floor lounge, lazy venom wafting up to her from the claims adjusters flopped on the couches on an extended smoke break. *Psycho bitch trying to kill those kids. You hear about that? Black ghetto crap. Could happen anywhere nowadays though. Anyfuckingwheres. They should castrate her. That's for dudes though. They do that for rapists in prison. Whatever. Razor blading little kids trying to have fun at the beach, fucking a. Nothing's sacred. Nothing. Psycho bitch. I like those words. This chick I went out with. No, no, for real, listen. This chick I went out with. Psycho bitch. Oh man, this guy lost skin from his right cheek in that crash they sent me the file on the other day. Lawyers are asking for a mil.*

She assigned daytime soap star faces to the voices, straining to hear the ebb and flow of the shit talk over two office assistants screeching at a dirty joke birthday card, reduced now, in this decade of her life, to terminal eavesdropper and wannabe hypochondriac. She'd just turned fifty-five and developed a series of aches and tics and outbursts that staked claim to a specific part of her body depending on the day of the week. Monday, tremors of the knee that she spent hours researching on the web. Black homing device floaters that soared in and out of vision on Thursday Sig Alerts. Aversions to the glopped on cheddar cheese of the cafeteria tuna melts that twinkled past from the display carousel on Fridays. Clockwork osmotic irregularity on Saturday mornings. She paid a hundred bucks a month in co-pays for doctor visits, and it was all the same. She'd become overly acquainted with the snot-colored floral patterns of her HMO's waiting rooms, the wheezing complaints of neurasthenic patients, the loping circuit of the hospital shuttle disgorging men with oxygen masks at the main entrance every half hour. Each time, she held her breath for the ritual of pressure taken, weight recorded, urine sample schlepped by a battery of gum smacking nurses, murderous when no special diagnosis was made to keep her company at night.

Following Kat's case had kept her distracted from her body's mutiny, the silent steady descent into unbeing. When the first alarm went off in the morning, she hit the snooze button and fell back asleep, drooling through a recurring dream of driving past herself slumped over the steering wheel of her car on the shoulder of a crowded freeway. She would rot for days until the atomic stench brought out the highway patrol. The car would be impounded into the netherworld of police auctions, then parceled out as graveyard scrap when there were no takers, sliding down into a mountain of nightmare road dismemberments waiting for the bloodhound nose of the right mechanic. Her cockeyed shot at immortality, the congealed crust of her holding together the chassis of a 200,000 mile beater. She fantasized that death would come slow and feline, coyly disguised in a stray sneeze from an adjoining cubicle, an after-dinner peppermint wrapped by a malarial factory worker, bits of ground up rat tail in a hotdog at an August baseball game. Slow as molasses in January feline, licking its fur into a halogen gleam that mocked her lifelong avoidance of risk and personal attachment, thumbed its nose at her faithfulness to routine. It would come dandified and stinkingly banal, an evening's final snapshot of her scrambling for change, waiting to have a bag of frozen peas scanned at a grocery check stand as the last bomb fell.

Truth was, she envied Kat's balls. Had always envied them, even when her stomach churned with contempt for her butter melting, fake countrified accent or her artless ingratiation with the old horny bachelors she'd tried to scam out of their retirements in her third act as a boiler room telemarketer. She had a certain cockroach-after-Armageddon hardiness to her that drove Riley wild. If she could hold onto Kat's cape when the big death came, they'd both still be standing. She played the perp walk in her head, over and over in her own private orgasmic loop, while she entered velocity dimensions onto a spreadsheet, the rhythm driving her through the cavernous leap from four to six in the afternoon. When there was a lull in the foot traffic of clerks and bike messengers and wanderers that streamed past her cubicle, she wrote a letter to Kat, eking out a few sentences, tearing it up because it sounded like the stupidest, mealy mouthed, pen pal kind of shit.

She was unwilling to accept the whole thing as a sign of Kat's madness. Unwilling to believe it was anything other than a tiny, calculated act of insurrection, a grand scheme that had been germinating ever since they'd first met bussing tables at summer camp. Kat had asked her to be the lookout when she laced the head cook's beefsteak sandwich with pop rocks, explosives to avenge his butt pinching of the girls on kitchen patrol.

A few weeks after she was incarcerated, Kat came up missing from the women's prison downtown. The news stations interviewed the neighbors next door to the house she grew up in, setting up camp for two hours on the gray flat street of stucco hell bungalows, the cameras panning across the blur of cornrowed little girls weaving in and out of the driveways with their bikes. On each station, the white reporter or the token Black or Latino trotted out for the voyage gave a curt summary of the beach sandbox invasion, gestured stiffly to the facade of the house and speculated on her whereabouts. Channel 6 cornered an elderly woman with a shopping cart, pumping her for a few minutes, until she snarled, "I don't know, and I don't care. Ya'll only come down here whenever something bad happens, damn vultures."

The rubberneck Nintendo slut in the cubicle next to Riley's caught her watching the news on her tiny screen TV the second day of the search. Every day, a new car crash, a new voyeur's adventure. The rubberneck hoarded his fingernail clippings out of fear the DNA would be confiscated and used to build a case for a future crime he might commit accidentally. There are stealth collectors everywhere, paid by the ounce. A lucrative side hustle for the underemployed, the bio-aspirational jonesing for dead skin cells. The rubberneck prides himself on his slacker routine of diddling with his hard drive when a supervisor walks by, slurping on a Diet Coke, launching into a snorting laugh that travels time zones. After eight months, she had him down to a science. Knows his break time, his lunch time, his crap time. Knows the exact beat when he'd lurch forward from his desk chair, circumnavigating the hallway to the bathroom, deliberating over every step. She keeps earplugs ready to protect herself from the westward splatter of the laugh whenever he scores a jump shot on his pocket basketball game or talks on his cell phone, relishing his role as the company's grand vizier of time wasting.

He drapes himself over the wall of her cubicle and squints as the newscast turns to the "manhunt" for the Halloween candy terrorist.

"They're upping the reward on that you know," he says.

"That so?"

"It's all over the news. They're offering like five thousand dollars more on top of the fifteen thousand dollars they already kicked in."

She nods and continues watching the TV. He hovers, scratching his armpits. A Fruit Loops commercial comes on. Kids bounce off a jungle gym and into an airbrushed kitchen, shoveling multicolored sugar scuds into their mouths.

"Aww, sweet. That's what I had for dinner last night," he says. "But seriously, sure would like to find out a way to get in on some of that easy money. That would solve a whole shitload of problems for me."

She misspells a word on her keyboard, banging on the backspace key to try and ward off further comment, but he keeps standing there, moth to the flame of her indifference. He takes a soggy Cup Noodles soup package out of his jacket pocket and tears the lid off.

"Ton of fucking student loans. Like, major interest accruing every second on these fucking student loans. Like, *tick, tick, tick* in my head. You got any?"

"Yeah.

"Paid 'em off yet?"

"That's a forward question."

"Yeah? I figured you might have some insight into that kind of thing. Like, how to get up from under this interest noose."

"I got none whatsoever."

The breaking news jingle comes on.

"Aww, sweet. More beef. C'mon, let's hear it, goons."

The newscaster drones on about a series of carjackings in neighboring Orange County. Riley holds her breath, hoping Kat's mug wouldn't appear on-screen again as the rubbernecker perks up, readying his soup for the microwave.

"Now that shit's spread to the O.C. Real messed up. L.A.'s infecting everything big-time."

"Heard the suspect was from Anaheim," Riley lies. "Drove off in a Pluto suit."

"Don't dis Pluto. He's one of my favorites." He smirks, nose damp with a pending sniffle. "My interest rate went up to fifteen percent this month. Gougers want you to default."

He sticks his finger into the blob of noodles, licks the salt off, and disappears behind the cubicle partition. Video game bleeps ascend into the air.

After that, she takes the TV into the women's bathroom to avoid him. She is one of the few women on a floor of a dozen bio-technology and engineering companies. She spends ten minutes of the first part of her lunch checking the noon top of the hour news summaries, ignoring the two or three pert, ponytailed lab techs who glide in self-importantly in their white smocks for zit inspections before hitting the cafeteria. They rant about dumb supervisors, fucked up car payments, ugly cipher guys trying to hit on them, dead-end weekends, all the while flipping their hair into the sink drains in greasy bunches. They scrape mascara from the corners of their eyes and bare their teeth, searching for grit leftover from breakfast, oblivious as zoo animals.

Then they leave in a lather of industrial strength perfume, grunting and slurring in white dialect thicker than any kind of Ebonics, shaking their heads at the pathetic little TV. Outside, the halls vibrate with workers massing at the elevators for lunch, a turbine whoosh of Palms and Pods and cells clicking in code. She unplugs the TV, sticks it into her bag, and waits for the ping of the elevator signal, until the last door closes and the hall is empty.

She takes the stairs down to the atrium, soothed by the cool austerity of the underused stairwell. If a bomb hits the building, she will already be halfway down to the street, calmly wending her way through the hordes of skittering, bleeding tech drones while the coke Super Sippers and Twinkie inhalers, too lazy to take the stairs, got religion in the dark of the sweatbox elevators. Sitting ducks.

When she was eight, she remembered seeing a picture from Dresden with a staircase poking out of smoking rubble, the steps twisted against the skyline like a ribcage. She stared at it for a long time in fascination, searching the page for bodies. On the fifth floor, the walls brimmed with graffiti, messages in a bottle from sixty years before when the building was a train terminal surging with passengers waiting for the tracks to click for the next local.

On the fourth floor, it stinks of cat pee. On the third, she stops to catch her breath, cursing the chili fries she got from a drive-through the night before. She bends down for a moment, breathing through her nose. A shadow passes over the wall from someone coming up from the second floor.

"Hi, Riley," a voice says.

It's Kat, with a pea coat slung over her shoulder. She teeters on the step, smiling, thinner than on TV, the baby fat face of summer camp sucked up into the cove of her cheekbones.

"K-Kat, what are you doing here?"

She runs her hand along the banister, inspecting the stairwell.

"Looking for bugs, listening devices. They broke the news about that government wiretapping madness, and nobody Black said anything about it."

"I wouldn't say nobody."

"Shit-for-brains Negro leaders is nobody."

She reaches into the jacket and takes out a pocketknife. She shines the tip of the knife with spit from her finger, then digs into the wall.

"They're like landmines. There's a special art to finding them."

Riley watches her scrape at the old faded paint, straining to hear if the stairwell door is opening.

"Heard you escaped from jail."

Kat keeps scraping.

"That's what *they* say."

"How'd you do it?"

"I walked my ass out of there."

She's managed to dig a half-inch hole in the wall. The floors upstairs echo with people coming back from lunch. She steps back and looks at the hole.

"How long have you worked for these fuckers?"

"About two years."

"Contract worker?"

"Yeah. A few months more on probation before they make me permanent."

Kat laughs. "A two year probation? You're on fantasy island. What's the pay like?"

"Passable. They're going to be looking for you—"

"I tried calling you all last week. You didn't answer. Don't you have voicemail?"

Riley pauses and stares at the hole. Something like honey or semen is dripping out of it.

"I know your routine. You get up at five thirty in the morning, ride the bus on Thursdays, drive the other four days, work with a bunch of no necks, live in an apartment building that's all medical offices. I've got your little routine down cold."

Riley clenches her fist in her pocket, hoping no one will pop into the stairwell.

"Little routine?"

"Too lowly for the government to wiretap."

"Yep, that's right, and you're the big-balled fugitive. What're you doing here, Kat?"

"Still got insomnia?"

"Why?"

"What wakes you up?"

Riley hesitates. Break time is over. Two more minutes, and the line supervisor will amble through, slurping a lukewarm cup of coffee and doing a beady-eyed reconnaissance for who's in the cubicles.

"The racetrack across the street. Trucks loading out the horses, banging, making noise. Anything, really."

"Horse neighs, that's some insidious shit."

"Kat, you have to get out of here. My job—"

"Bet the looming cubicle keeps you awake. Got any pictures of me, of us in it? Singing campfire songs from the olden days?"

"I've got to get back."

"Oh, silly me. I guess you would've taken those down already, what with this latest development. Don't want anyone knowing about our past."

Riley lowers her voice. "Latest development? You're calling what you did a 'development'?"

"What they *said* I did. Nobody's got any proof."

"Look, you need money?"

"Insomnia. Wonder what the etymology of that word is. Would look it up, but nobody uses dictionaries these days. Paper is fucked. You dream in little sections?"

"All dreams are in sections. Sleep stages."

"If someone put a gun to your head and forced you, which stage would you choose to be stranded in?"

Kat digs into the bottom of the wall, latticed with mildew from leaking pipes, decades-old excretions of all the bodies that passed through the stairwell since it was built.

Riley takes a step toward her. "C'mon, stop that shit. There's nothing planted in there—"

"How do you know? I asked you a simple question—"

"I need to get back to my desk—"

"Cubicle."

"Workspace."

"You're a rat in a cage. Hamster on a wheel."

"The R.E.M. stage, satisfied?"

"That's a cliché. Everybody says that 'cause they don't know what the other ones are. R.E.M. or Delta, that's where all the nasty stuff happens. The big death. See, all the others leading up to it—teeny, like, fucking Lilliputian. You get stuck in Delta, you'll never get out."

Riley grabs the knife from her. "Stop it! You're fucking it up even more for yourself!"

Footsteps echo above them. File clerks bound down, clutching cigarette packs, gabbing about crashing a reality show audition down the street. Kat flattens herself upon the wall to let them pass, mouthing the word "boo" to their shiny stick figure faces.

They ignore her and keep going, giggling, trilling "hump day, hump day" out the door to the parking garage. Midweek, Wednesday, the jitteriness beginning.

"Saved by the bell," Kat says. She gestures to the knife. "You're going to want to give that back."

"No."

"Might be the assault weapon for all you know."

"Thought you said they were lying on you."

"They are. But how's that saying go? Better safe than sorry. I mean, my DNA is all over it. And now yours is too."

Riley looks down at her hand. The stairwell is still. Break time had ended. The torpid haze of late afternoon settles over the building. She rubs the knife handle off with her sleeve and gives it back to Kat.

She takes it and puts it in her jacket pocket. "You always were real smart. I didn't dream the night before the cops picked me up. I was driving around, looking for something to eat for two hours. Sunday. City was deader than dead. Drove through Hawthorne. Dead as shit strip malls full of nail salons and liquor stores. Stopped at a three for one taco stand and got me some fish tacos. Hot sauce, pink sauce, shredded lettuce, best in the world. Was down to the crumbs when this white girl with these two little kids hanging off her like a clothesline comes up begging for change. Thinking like, what the fuck is fifty cents gonna get her with those hungry urchins grinding her tits to dust? At any given moment, see, somebody would've come out of the woodwork and handed her a million-dollar lottery ticket. Dumb me offered to buy her and the kids a taco instead. Girl gets an attitude at first, then accepts just right when the whole shit-for-brains neighborhood busts in for tacos. Place is closing, smells like a slaughterhouse, cooks falling all over each other, scraping mystery meat off the grill. One of the white girl's kids comes up with this razor blade and a bite-sized Snickers, asked me to cut it in half. We were just playing a game, see."

"So, you got framed."

"Like I said, I tried calling you all week. Needed a character witness."

"You got framed."

"Yeah."

"You're lying."

"Scout's honor."

"You're lying. You didn't call me. Plus, I heard it happened near Hermosa, not Hawthorne. Million-dollar difference."

"Somebody who sounded like you picked up the number I called."

"Thought you said nobody answered. I've got to get back to work."

"Whoever it was had a whiny voice like yours."

"Did she tell you that you shouldn't have fucked with those kids?"

"Nobody fucked with them. It was just a game. They instigated it."

Riley grasps the banister, struggling to command herself to put one foot in front of the other. She needs to get out while there is still a chance and is grateful the company is too cheap to put cameras in the stairwells. She tries to keep her eyes off the hickey on Kat's neck, the way it spreads out and up from the collar of her dirty T-shirt, pranking her, mocking her with its off-red juiciness.

She wonders for a jealous split second about who gave it to her. *Jailbird quickie? Dry hump desperado?* Her stomach reels at the thought of Kat devolved into a petty disgrace to the race criminal, still getting some, waking up from her stupid-ass preferred sleep stage all googly-eyed and sated. Kat saw her looking at the hickey and straightened her shoulders.

"This? They kicked my ass. A Black chick who thought she was white led the charge. After they confiscate your shit, they go through every hole in your body and ream it like you're a fucking animal. I was throwing up for two hours, mashed into a cell with five other people."

"So how did you escape?"

She laughed. "My big-time escape from Alcatraz? Carved a gun from soap, repelled all the pigs in one fell swoop."

"Who gave you that hickey?"

"It's a mosquito bite. That all you care about? I just told you they practically killed me."

"If you came in with an attitude, you deserved it."

"All of us Negroes did."

"Right. C'mon, Kat—"

"So the ladies I was in the holding cell with found out who I was and what I supposedly did, and it was like they went into judge, jury, and executioner mode. Amazing. A bunch of crackheads and meth heads and kleptos, getting high on feeling high and mighty. You know how there's this food chain in prisons, men's at least, with the rapists and the pedophiles down on the hell rungs."

"Please, you have to go."

"It was forty-eight hours of torture with two so-called sistas, trading scripture, seeing who could throw down the longest and loudest to get God to have mercy on my trifling soul. Both of them just itching to do an exorcism. Cast out the demon and see it fry on the ground right in front of them. All for a little white shit that lied on me. Negroes just love them some white babies—"

"Bullshit! You got in there and started shooting your mouth off and looking down your nose at everybody, and that's why they stomped you. Now, in addition to whatever you get for messing with that white kid, you'll get time for running—"

"I can vanish. Slip through the cracks. A white man killed his whole family, disappeared, surfaced in some hick town, and started a whole new life with another woman for decades before the feds found him."

Riley got in her face. "*They* can do that. You know that."

"Yeah, I know… Will you help me?" The knife glints in her hand. She presses it into the tip of her finger, making a red point of raised skin.

"Don't," Riley says.

"Will you help me?" The door on the fourth floor wheezes open. Coughs, nervous laughter cascade down. A party whistle blows.

"They framed me," she whispers. "You know it."

"I-I don't know shit—"

"Whose fucking side are you on?"

"I'm not on a side. I just need to get back, just need to keep this fucking job... Some asshole in claims is having a birthday. They're doing a raffle. I have a ticket. It's a small office. They're going to come look for me. Maybe even write me up."

Riley thinks of the elastic bodies of rats, tiny skeletons bending and twisting to penetrate any opening. She read somewhere that there were now twenty rats for every human on the planet. Whole underground kingdoms seething in subway stations across the globe, waiting for a ripe moment for insurrection. With a rat's skeleton, time travel would be easy. There are certain pressure points that can be slipped through, parallel universes shifting underfoot, soft and lumpy like the unfused meridians of a baby's head.

"Be on my side, and I'll help you keep the job. See, the key is the Delta stage."

"Just go, *please*."

"Can I crash at your place for a day?"

"No."

"Why?"

"You know why."

"For a night then."

"One hour, one night, it doesn't matter. I still can't do it. Don't you fucking understand? This is the first good shot I've had at earning a retirement beyond the peanuts I'll get with Social Security. I can't fuck this up..."

Kat nodded slowly, her bottomless eyes softening for a beat. "Right. I saw online you had a bankruptcy a few years ago." She handed Riley the knife. "Here. Keep it for when they come for you."

Riley stayed up most of the night, listening to passing cars outside her apartment, too wasted to cook or microwave. She settled for saltines and Velveeta for dinner, eating ten crackers for every car that went by. Security guards, janitors, and cooks walked from the bus stop to the racetrack, talking into their flip phones, hustling through the gates to clock in on time for their shifts.

The rhythm and discipline of waiting, eating, waiting took her mind off the incident with Kat for a bit. She was afraid to sleep, knew she'd be stalked in a dream. Caught in the downy smoothness of Kat's Dorian Gray skin shining under the stairwell light. Her bottomless eyes suspended over Riley's cubicle as campfire crackled in the distance.

At 1:30 a.m., someone knocked on the door. She'd left the TV on. A juicer infomercial buzzed on the screen, touting vim, vigor, stamina, rejuvenation, an elixir in a Super Sipper cup for three installments of $10.99.

Riley peered through the front window at Kat pacing by the door, her jacket hanging limply off her matchstick frame.

"Freezing out here. C'mon, I know you're there. Got a present for you."

Riley weighed her options. If they argued, the racetrack workers might hear. If she let Kat in, the closed-circuit cameras would pick it up. Either way, she was fucked.

Kat knocked again. "Fingers are getting numb," she rasped.

Riley cracked open the door. "Keep it down."

"Can I come in?"

Riley stepped back.

"Thanks," Kat said.

"What's the present?"

"Got anything decent to eat?"

"Odds and ends."

Kat walked over to the cupboard, peering in at the jumble of half open cracker boxes.

"Time for a restock."

"You got five minutes."

"Five minutes before what? Here."

She pulled out a balled up blue rag from her jacket and handed it to Riley.

"What's this?"

"A little artifact."

Riley opened it. Numbers had been spray-painted into the cloth.

"Remember how proud you were to get that? I didn't get one because of the fight I was in."

"You were never in a fight. I was. I defended you from those assholes stealing tampons from your bunk."

She paused. "You're right. Don't know how I misremembered that. Anyway, if I recall correctly, the brown-nosing shits in their first year at camp got this for living up to good Christian values and pledging fealty to God."

"So that's the real reason you didn't get one."

"I accept Satan as my Lord and personal savior."

"Don't say that."

"I never thanked you for saving the day."

"No big deal."

"It *was* a big deal." They fell silent. "I drove up there a few weeks ago. Our cabin's still there."

"Oh, yeah?"

"All the other ones burned down, though. Nothing but charred woods around cabin fifteen, like the last man standing. And that bathroom where the boys spied on us when we peed? That's gone too."

She took some crackers from the plate Riley had left on the counter.

"You ever set anything on fire before?"

"No."

"I think some of those girls, those holier-than-thou, Jheri juice assholes, were pyros."

She blew on her hands. "What I wouldn't give for a roaring fire right now. Shit, L.A. shouldn't be this cold."

"Three minutes."

"Five."

"I have to go to work in an hour."

"Nobody saw shit. I disabled the cameras... Put the rag on."

"You put it on. Looks like a fucking noose now."

"In a manner of speaking, it was."

"What do you mean, you disabled the cameras?"

Kat took the rag from her and tried to tie it around her neck. Riley jerked away, avoiding the bottomless eyes, her tininess reflected in them. "Stop it!"

"You don't have to be skittish around me. You weren't back then. I was the skittish one. The one trying to get away from the hook—"

"There was never any hook."

"That's right. You were more tender than that."

"How did you disable the camera?"

"Gum and a cold cock."

Riley grabbed the rag, shaking it at her. "This shit isn't funny, Kat. What the fuck did you do to the camera??"

"They can't spy on us now."

"The landlords look at that shit every twenty-four hours."

"Calm down. Put the rag on—"

"No."

"Pretty please, sugar on top."

"Will you leave if I do?"

"If that's what you really want."

Riley hesitated, then put it on. The first bus of the morning stopped outside, pausing to let out passengers, closing its doors, wheezing forward into the darkness.

"Beautiful," Kat said. "Goes good with your hair."

She took out a mirror and held it up to Riley's face. "You're a vision."

"The only thing's left from our old cabin, 4B, I think it was, is the window frame."

"Thought you said it'd burned down."

"That's right. I did say that. Anyway, we used to look out at the lake from that window from my top bunk."

"Wrong again. You slept on the bottom because you wet the bed at home. Didn't want to risk being *pee girl* in the middle of night."

"That's a lie."

"The hell it is… This thing reeks of that old bunk bed."

"I just washed it."

"In the lake?"

Kat grinned. "At the laundromat."

"Remember how you were afraid to swim?"

"I was never afraid to swim. I was the best swimmer in the whole—"

"That story about ghosts at the bottom, grabbing at your feet. The ghost of a baby that got thrown out of a rowboat. Baby fingers tickling at the bottom of your—"

"Shut up."

"Some kids pretending like they was massa, manning a slave ship. They threw a white baby overboard just to see if it could float—"

"I could do a butterfly stroke; nobody else in the whole camp could do a butterfly stroke."

"Got any matches on you?"

"What for?"

She made a move toward Kat. "To light this stove. Give me the matches that you used to burn the cabin down."

Kat backed up into the counter. "Now you're trying to frame me. I was clear on the other side of the country when that happened."

"You said you were cold. It'll be warmer in here with the stove on. We can make believe it's a campfire."

Kat scrunched in the counter, searching Riley's face, inches from her now. "I don't casually carry matches on me. Back up."

"This is my place, remember?"

"That doesn't give you the right to—"

Riley dug her hands into Kat's front pocket, pulling out a damp book of matches. "My lucky day. One left. Looks like it's too wet to use, though. What's it dipped in? Blood or gasoline?"

"Give it back."

She squinted at the cover of the matchbook. "Don't think so. I'll keep them as a memento of our visit. Greetings from the Grove Motel. Nice stay? Sleep well?" She sniffed it. "Gas. Figures. That flea bag right off Route 6, a few miles from camp, right? The only one that accommodated spooks back in the day."

"Give it back."

"What was the last match for?"

"Nothing."

"That the real reason why you showed up here? To set this building on fire? That why you disabled the camera?"

"No."

"I always wondered what pyros got out of burning up forests and shit."

"You tell me."

"They say it's something sexual, right? The bigger the flame, the bigger the climax. Makes perfect sense. Although you never had the backbone to do anything more than that little trash can fire you set to roust the camp counselors out of the lake and set the alarm off."

"I had more backbone than all of you. They were bullies and thugs. Anybody who so-called got out of line had to freeze their asses off, collecting pinecones in their panties at midnight."

"Fucking sadists."

"They were gonna target you. The mellow, high yellow campfire's object of desire."

"And you were my knight in shining armor."

"Wasn't I? The whole world was supposed to be jealous of you. Even the dead ones supposedly at the bottom of the lake."

"Right, they woke me up with their pissing and moaning. And there was no 'supposedly' about it."

"I defended you against all of them."

"You're delusional."

"You never acknowledged it. Not once."

Riley reached for her purse. "I got forty dollars on me. Take it and go."

"I don't want the money. They're nickel and diming you at that punk job. Last hired, first fired, remember? I don't want your chump change."

"Take it and go."

"They called me everything except a child of God."

"Who?"

"All they really wanted was to fuck you."

"Take it."

"Fronting with their little second-hand boyfriends—"

"Sick."

"Tone's a smidge underwhelming. You like that, huh? Deep down. Makes you wet? What I wouldn't give for some marshmallows now for this fire we're about to set. Oh shit, I rhymed. I'm a fucking poet."

Riley snatched the matchbook from the counter as Kat grinned, grabbing Riley's purse. "It's just a metaphor," she said. "That itty-bitty damp match couldn't—"

"Give it back."

"No."

"You're going to make me late for work—"

"You should've thought about that before you let me in... All I wanted to do was talk, spend a little time. That's all. Like, maybe put on that rag again, and we could fly away from here."

"Yeah, our magic carpet. Fly away and go find those kids you messed with. Find 'em and apologize—"

"Fuck those motherfuckers. Where's my apology for the lies they're telling about me all over the news? There's a place in the woods I found. A mile away from camp. You can see clear to the next country practically."

"Sounds like bliss—"

"Let's go then."

Kat had thrown up once after watching some girls from another cabin suck the blood out of the finger blisters they got from a ropes course. Five of them, stone bored, flopping like landlocked guppies in the summer sun, trying to outgross each other. Double daring to see who was the most badass before the voodoo doll arts n' crafts session that afternoon. Slurping up each other's secrets, lies, nightmares to become someone else for an hour, floating downstream into the subterranean biota of their esophagi; the sharp tang of blood on their tongues taking them to the moon. Riley had helped Kat go to the camp nurse, pukey and ashamed. She'd begged her not to tell anybody. Afraid she'd be shipped back home to the apartment she shared with the stoner great aunt who was always trying to rent her room out to new boarders anyway.

"Let's go then," Kat said again, the desperation in her voice a pearl gleaming from an oyster shell.

"How would we get there?" Riley heard herself asking, squeezing the lighter in her left hand.

"Your car. Or maybe that dumb shit in the cubicle next to yours can drive us. He wants to bone you, the dirty little mutt."

"In his insomniac dreams."

"Could save gas."

"What do I need to bring?"

"A change of underwear, toothpaste, toothbrush, a bathing suit for the lake, a telescope for the stars. Guarantee you'll be able to see that planet I named after you in 1983."

Riley started to go to her bedroom. Kat followed. The apartment had shrunk since Kat had come in. She breathed, dry, deep, fetal. The first doomed point-of-no-return gasps slapped from the womb.

"Stay there," she said, turning to face Kat. "I haven't had anyone in there, in here, in years."

Kat smiled. "Now's the time to break it in."

"I said, stay."

Kat hesitated. "What've you got in there?"

"Nothing."

"Then let me help you."

"Remember how you were afraid of the water?"

"I was never afraid of the water. You get middle-aged and your memory goes to shit."

"Never where you're concerned."

"I was the best damn swimmer in the camp. Nobody can take that away from me."

"That's open to debate."

"Fuck that, I nearly rescued you a few times when you couldn't do the laps test."

"True. That doesn't mean you weren't afraid."

"What did I have to be afraid of?"

Riley opened the door to her room, turning to face Kat. She unfolded the rag. They stood level with each other. "Here, put this on over your eyes."

"Why?"

"It's the magic carpet, remember?"

"What?"

"Put it on, and we'll go back to the woods. We won't need a car."

Kat hesitated. "You're fucking kidding."

"No."

"Riley…"

Riley paused, then broke into a smile. "Sure had you going there for a moment though."

"Yeah."

"You wanted to believe it, though, right? Just like you wanted to believe there's been some deep, dark bond between us that brought you here."

"What's in your room?"

"You see, I happen to know that you got dumped."

"The room, what's in it?"

"Left for dead on the bottom of the lake."

"I asked you—"

"Burned to a crisp in that fire because you tried to shit on God."

"Now you're talking crazy."

"That Kat. The Kat I knew, back then, died before she saw twenty."

"Stop it."

"And I envied her."

"Stop."

"Forever young."

"Back up—"

"Released from all these decades of war and Armageddon and being in debt up to your eyeballs—"

"I said—"

"And marking time, most of all. Getting up, going to bed, eating, crapping, walking through quicksand, watching the world go to shit around you, helpless to stop it, just marking time—"

"Come with me, and it'll be better, I promise. That's why I came back here."

"Why should I believe you?"

"How many years have we known each other?"

"Kat died before twenty."

"Don't say that."

"You asked what was in my room."

Kat paused. Outside, the din of passing cars, swinging entry gates, and idling buses had receded, giving way to a dull white hiss. She leaned forward, listening. Under the floorboards, between the walls, insects were gnawing, dragging their dead into hives. She could hear every minor creep and deliberation, every budding bug conspiracy. She could feel their patience as they waited to pounce, soothing each other, antennae laced with human skin.

"Get your stuff," she whispered. "If we leave now, we can beat traffic."

Riley nodded. She went into her room and came out with a jar, grasping it tightly in her fist. "Kat. The real Kat's ashes. No one in her family wanted to claim them, so I became their caretaker of sorts."

Kat stepped back, the hiss building to a roar. "We can take the 10 freeway. This time of the morning, the diamond lane will move, get us to San Bernardino in an hour and change—"

Riley opened the jar and pushed it into Kat's face. "Want to smell? Death at twenty has a certain odor."

"Get that away from me—"

"Where's your backbone now? Kat was fearless."

"She is, *I am*, still fearless."

"She stood up to all those bullies and ghosts on the bottom of the lake until she died."

"What the fuck? You're talkin' crazy. Put that shit away and let's go."

"Listen to you. You can barely keep your accents straight. I told Kat a few secrets."

"The longer we wait, the worse it's going to be on the drive—"

"Name one."

"I don't know, you said a lot of things—"

"Imposter!"

"Ok, then… You watched your cousin nearly bleed to death after he busted his head falling off a pogo stick."

"Imposter."

"You thought it was funny. Remember that?"

"Liar."

"Mumbling in your sleep, tossing and turning in the top bunk the second night of camp."

Riley pushed the jar back into her face. "Smell it!"

Kat snatched it from her, sending it crashing to the floor. It broke, a tiny cloud of dust rising around their feet.

"Jesus," Kat said. "Where'd you get this fake shit from anyway?"

"You lied."

"Here, let me help clean it up."

Riley gestured to an empty sugar bowl on the counter. "Sweep it up, and put it in that. There's a broom in the closet over there."

Kat hesitated. "I'm sorry."

"Save it."

"You've been harboring shit against me all these years. Where'd you get the crazy idea I was dead?"

"Just get the broom, please."

"Stop bossing me."

"Sweep Kat up, and put her in the sugar bowl."

"This some kind of sick fantasy of yours?"

"I don't want to leave the place a mess while we're gone."

"So, you're coming with me?"

A bus horn blasted outside.

Riley nodded. "Give me a moment. I'll get my stuff."

She went into her room and shut the door. She opened her nightstand drawer and took out a gun, listening to the whoosh of the broom against the kitchen floor.

She picked up the phone on her nightstand and dialed.

A woman's voice greeted her on the other line. She cleared her throat softly, in a low campfire song tone.

"Operator, I'm at 9500 Prairie. There's an intruder in my apartment. Goes by the name Kat. She's wanted… Yes, that one… armed and dangerous."

The Delirium

ALL WEEK, THE CHILDREN HAD been promised a treat. Apple-cheeked and manic, they resolved to be good. Especially Grayson, who had never won anything before. Even when recess had been declared abolished and the rain dribbled down the school windowpanes like bug grease smashed on a car grill, they'd made a pact among one another to be obedient, lest one miscreant muck it up for everyone.

Last week's treat had been chocolate ice cream, seasoned with crystalline bits of ground glass. Barely detectible to the digestive tract. An evolutionary test.

"It would pass out easily with your poop," Dillinger said, as she picked a storybook from the top shelf, flipped through it, frowned, and put it back, holding forth about the powers of elimination. A silverfish skittered onto her hand and up the sleeve of her coat. It was the third time Grayson had seen that happen. Was there some secret pact, some alliance between the species and Dillinger? Grayson wondered whether Dillinger would ever read to them like the teacher they had before. Then she wondered about the fate of the bug and what Dillinger did when they were all fast asleep and the children were adrift, together again at long last, on the hurtling train. There were ten of them now. Up from six. Six was the number of the beast, Dillinger had said, although Grayson secretly didn't believe in hellfire and damnation.

When they dumped the dirt on you, you went back down into the bacterial hum before birth. And that was that.

The children buzzed about the treat during bathroom breaks and dodge ball. The ten minutes they had for recreation, grooming, and small talk; the coveted moments during a long day of cramming formulas, figures, and stats. Whoever was hall monitor would get two extra minutes of leave. Dillinger rotated the position, never playing favorites, except, sometimes, with EM, short for Elephant's Memory.

EM never spoke, except to titter about the treat. Hyping, coaxing, posing—animal, mineral, or vegetable in a high-pitched squeal that punched through the roof to the fudgesicle sky. They wondered how someone so tiny could be so loud. How such a weakling could go for hours on end without food, slaughter everyone in dodge ball, burble like interplanetary radio. How a piker could still master the formulas Dillinger drilled them on, backward and forward, without a calculator or a pencil. At night, the children crawled into her bed and thumped her to see if she had a circuit board in her back. Praying that Dillinger wouldn't get up to do inspections or take a long, luxurious shit, scribbling her lesson plans on poison ivy palms rubbed raw.

EM had arrived a month ago from another school and taken the place of a child who had been kicked out. At first, the children marveled at her wittiness, her spit polish fingernails. How she seemed gobs smarter than Dillinger. When the novelty faded, they wrote her off as a teacher's pet, curiosity sliding into contempt.

Except for Grayson. EM intrigued her. When the children closed their eyes and settled into sleep, she saw her hovering, one foot in consciousness and Dillinger's jackhammer world of homework and drills, the other in the Delirium. In the second car of the hurtling train.

Grayson looked at EM's snow blond hair frizzing in the steam of the old radiator. If the children's hair was a centimeter off regulation length, it would be hacked off. If there was too much wax in their ears, they would be boxed. If their nails curled into talons, they'd be clipped and put in the school safe for tracking. Nail clippings carried the imprint of movement, whereabouts, intent. They knew that code transgressions were always lurking in the teeniest detail. That flouters would stay in the valley of Dillinger's moist armpit until they cried uncle. That flouters could be banished to Solitary, banned from the Delirium.

Descending into the Delirium, they could only speculate on when and where the treat would be provided. Sitting in the same seats they'd sat in for the first ride and the twentieth and the two thousandth. Freeways, gas stations, mini marts, houses knocking by in black anonymity. The maw of unfinished buildings, beams aglow in the streetlights. Auto graveyards snaking to the sky with burnt carcasses. The intercom bleating above them, their heads throbbing with the effort to understand the words. They knew each grind, each ping, each *click-clack* on the tracks by heart, watched the riders in the first car hungrily. On some nights, there'd be a lone passenger, hunched over a newspaper, gnawing at a Twinkie, stabbing their ear with a toothpick, finger reading the route map overhead. On other nights, there would be a roving, grunting mass, backs to them, speaking in tongues as the conductor stumbled through, passing out tickets. Dillinger's commands would drill bit into their frontal lobes. Rise and shine. Carpe diem. Up and at 'em. Hurly-burly. The day panting forward. Prayers. Breakfast. Recitations. Jumping Jacks. Silent reading. Pop quizzes. Wind sprints around the quad. One-minute showers. Inspections. Supper. List collation. There was beauty in routine. Mystery in routine. The secrets of the universe were in the dendrite crunching kamikaze of routine. It toughened the carapace and stiffened the spine.

Still, the treat dangled over their heads. Shiny. Mouthwateringly out of reach.

Once, they saw the stick figure profile of the woman in the first train car, her nose buried in a bouquet of lavender roses. The odor punched through the metal membrane to their car, tossed them back to the playground, to the rows of painted flowers just beyond the dodge ball circle. The withered buds watched them, ripe with the blood of all their smashing, crashing games. Rumor had it that Dillinger buried their nail clippings there, coaxing a harvest of new recruits at the end of the year. Children that were them and not them. Golems fanning out into the world, searching for hosts.

Each night, they spent more time in the Delirium. Quicker to get to sleep, longer to wake, struggling when the morning alarm cannon went off in the quad. Settling back into the Delirium, it became a contest to see who would reach the door to the first car the fastest. The woman's lavender roses teased and titillated like skeleton sails bobbing on the water, disappearing into the intercom voice babbling a blue streak.

Every afternoon, EM quizzed them about their time in the Delirium, eyes lashed with feline envy, scavenging for any minor detail that could let her in.

"Why can't I join?" she asked one day, sidling up to Grayson in the bathroom.

"It's not a club."

"If I close my eyes and think real hard, I'll get there."

"That's not how it works."

"How does it work, then? Tell me!" EM's voice rose, bouncing off the walls.

"No. Truthfully, I don't really know how."

"You're lying."

"Why would I lie about that?"

"To keep me out." EM stared at Grayson in the mirror, lathering her hands with industrial pink soap. "You never liked me anyway." She knotted her hands together, soap oozing down her stiff white uniform. "You know, God punishes liars."

"What God?"

"God. Don't act stupid. He hears and sees everything you do."

"How do you know that?"

"I just do. Everybody does, stupid."

Grayson paused, wanting to pull EM's snow bunny hair out strand by strand. "This God you say sees and hears everything doesn't know about what happens when we sleep."

"Yes, He does."

"He knows every secret, good or bad?"

"I told you, yes."

"Why doesn't He let you go with us?"

"I guess He has his reasons."

"Or maybe He's punishing you."

EM frowned. "I didn't do anything."

"He knows every secret."

"I don't have any secrets from Him."

"How long have you been wishing something would happen to one of us so you could take our place?"

"Quit it. I don't wish that."

"I don't see Him coming to defend you."

"It-it… He doesn't work like that—"

"Why not? What good is He then? You're the stupid one. If He's not defending you, then He must be punishing you for wishing bad things on us."

"No!" EM shrieked.

"He knows what you did—"

"No, he doesn't—I mean, I didn't think those things—"

"It's no good telling me. He's the one you have to confess to. But, of course, if He's everywhere, he just heard that. I'm not the one who's gonna have you burn in hell for thinking evil."

"You said you didn't believe that stuff."

"Maybe you made me change my mind."

EM balled her fists at her sides. "Tell me what you do when you close your eyes."

"No."

"I'll tell you where Dillinger keeps her dirty magazines."

"Why would I want to know that?"

"Because you're curious."

"You don't know anything."

"You talk in your sleep, you know."

"Yeah? And what am I saying?"

EM smiled, pleased with herself. "That's my secret."

"You don't have any secrets on me."

"I do."

"Prove it."

"I know why you were brought here."

Grayson waited. A buzzing sound started up in her ear, as though something was hatching in her cochlea, struggling to get free.

EM's smile slid into a pucker. "January, after New Year's, six years ago. Remember? You were brought here to this special school, from a regular school."

Grayson stiffened. "That was then."

"Are you saying you're a better girl?"

They brought her there right around the time she was learning to read. Graduating from picture books to deciphering the unruly, slanting marks on the page of her phonics primer brimming with boys and girls that looked like EM's devil spawn. Proud of reading her first words out loud in front of a class of squirming six-year-olds. The pride curdling as her first grade teacher ripped her for slurring her words, for hiding behind the dewy blond pigtails of the plastic princess in front of her, too dumb and drooling to connect the dark marks to meaning. If you can read, you can tame the world, the teacher declared, tapping at Grayson to get her feet out of the aisle. She had marveled at the quasar gleam of her women's sized patent leather shoes. She'd always been big for her age; dubbed Sasquatch, Godzilla, Minotaur by the tittering minions jamming the sandbox at recess. In her mind, she ripped their guts out with a paring knife, swallowing them up like plankton, morphing into the monster they feared hid underneath their beds. Double daring them to lift the covers. Threatening the jump ropers in the playground that if they hit her and drew blood, a clone of her would spring up from the spilled drops and spirit them away.

If she spoke revenge, she could make it real. Would she be punished for it afterward in the universe that EM had invented, all smug in her fables about God, hellfire, damnation?

EM blinked and leaned into her, repeating, "I know why you're here. I saw the file on you. Dillinger had it out on the desk."

After regular school one day, Grayson had walked to the elevated train station same as always, waiting in the middle of the platform away from the fifth graders selling wolf tickets. Guitar playing buskers screeched about love and abandon over dirty dollar bill wads in half-empty instrument cases. She'd taken off the tight shoes to let her feet breathe. The fifth graders were too busy trashing a pot-bellied snot nose boy to tease her funky feet. Grayson relished having the pressure off her, craned to hear the boy get beat down as she stretched her left foot out to catch the putrid whoosh of the oncoming train. The kids ran to the edge of the platform, racing to be the first ones on, pushing a man with a cane out of the way. "Gonna get a window seat!" the ringleader shrieked. He thrust his boar's snout into the air, commanding the others to follow. The beat down boy leaped up from his defensive crouch and launched forward, tripping on Grayson's outstretched foot, sprawling onto the tracks and into the arms of the third rail.

She remembered the sizzle and scream. Then the silent film stampede as the transit police dragged her barefoot across the platform. She curled herself into an armadillo ball, trying to split the seconds into tinier and tinier islands of time, crisscrossing from beginning, middle, and end. Fantasizing she could edit out the moments before the boy fell onto the tracks by closing her eyes, pretending to be mute, willing herself back to the classroom's cocoon.

"I know what happened," EM said for the fourth time. "How did it feel?" she whispered. "Did part of you like it?"

She pointed her fingers at Grayson, backing her into the sink. She could see the mangy black hairs in her nostrils, pale temples shimmering with pearls of sweat.

"I think you liked it," she said quietly.

"No."

"You can't hide that sin."

"It was an accident."

"Who says what an accident is? You can't prove it. Only God can. And even if it was an accident, the boy you killed is dead and you can't bring him back to life. But he'll be with you forever and ever and ever, up here." She pointed to Grayson's head, making a cocking motion.

"You're just a dumb teacher's pet," Grayson hissed. She didn't want to risk waking the others, unsure where their allegiances lay. Who else knew about her past but had remained silent, waiting to use it against her in a strategic moment? To get in good with Dillinger, revel in Grayson roasting over a spit as she was interrogated?

EM's warning about God grew wings, fluttering over her in the stifling bathroom air. Had she wanted the beat down boy to die? Had a pocket of her plotted and planned, a rogue splinter of herself, tucked away, hidden from the light of day? Stage managing her movements until they converged with his?

EM lathered soap on her hands over the sink, humming:

Baa, baa, black sheep, have you any wool? Yes sir, yes sir, three bags full.

She trilled the last line, as though they were the only two living beings left in the world, and the ugly melody was their life raft. She turned the hot water on full blast, reaching for the cold.

Had she wanted the beat down boy to die? Had a pocket of her plotted and planned? Had he been in the Delirium the night before, one of the faceless passengers?

Grayson grabbed EM's hands, jamming them under the spigot of the scalding water to stop the humming.

She barely flinched. The humming continued.

Grayson stumbled backward. "What the fuck are you?! Why won't you shut up?"

"You'll never be able to shut me up." She snickered.

Grayson grabbed at the white blond tendrils, splitting her in two, then three, then four. Shards of her bounced onto the sink, ping-ponging onto the floor, congealing into a bite-size toy train that vroomed full speed ahead toward Grayson's feet. The front car, the midsection, the caboose was stamped with the hangdog frenzy of EM's expression.

She thought she smelled a flicker, a spark near the engine. Thought she heard the pixilated whimper of little voices behind bite-size windows. Thought she saw a Tasmanian devil blur of what they said was life passing in front of her eyes. But then it was over, the other children shaking her out of bed, screeching at her to go down with them to breakfast.

"I killed EM," she murmured. "I watched her go to pieces. I stood there, watched."

"Don't be dumb," one said, pounding a sugar cube into their oatmeal. "Elephant turd just came in."

And so, EM had, materializing in the second row, school uniform pressed, starched, and shimmering. She smiled and waved at Grayson.

Dillinger went to the podium.

"Happy to report most of you excelled on your exams. Happy to report that tidiness and order were maintained in the washrooms."

The room was quiet, save for the whoosh of passing cars outside of the cracked window. Grayson noticed that some had begun to slow, turning into the driveway, crawling up the stretch of uneven, untended pavement, finding a parking spot. There had never been actual adult visitors that she could remember. Children came and went, disgorged or scooped up by the aggregator bus.

"Happy to report that there will be tomato soup with grilled cheddar cheese for lunch."

A few of them perked up, careful not to look at each other or risk being singled out, a wave of surprise wafting through the room. *Was this the treat? The fishhook plummeting beneath the surface?* What could be more delectable, more coveted, warmer, and transporting on a cloudless day when there were hearses in the parking lot?

EM had seen them first, peeking out of the window as she sharpened her pencil to a poker point.

"Happy to report that Grayson has won the treat," Dillinger said, "for helping others, being courteous, and going to bed on time for the past week." She held a hat out with notecards to Grayson. "Take your pick."

She hesitated. The children paused as her fingers skimmed the cards and settled on a light purple one, the lavender of the woman's roses on the train. A key fell out of the card, identical to the keys on the conductor's belt.

"Read it out loud," Dillinger commanded.

The recess bell sounded. The children filed out of the room, footsteps thumping down the stairs and out into the driveway to the waiting hearses.

Grayson unfolded the card, squinting at the scribble. The key was to the first train car, it said. A passport to peace, to sleep, to a special, separate section of the Delirium.

"All aboard!" EM screamed.

Grayson felt her head getting heavier, the ground moving beneath her feet as she sunk into the Delirium, waiting to receive the treat, the intercom voice rising, sharp, lavender-toned, clear, reciting the exact time and place of her death. Mouthwateringly within reach.

Gift from God

STARING UP AT THE BABY rat-sized gap in the ceiling, she nick-named the abortion doctor Itchy. He scratched his left ear with a rubber-gloved, board-certified hand. A drop of her blood hung perilously from the lobe like a burned red earring. She monitored the clink of each medical instrument, the unused ones lined mil-itarily on the metal tray, lovingly swabbed and re-swabbed with rubbing alcohol.

She'd had a grade school crush on isopropyl. The sinus shred-ding malodorousness of it giving her a contact high. Sending her on ghost tippy-toes to the coatroom alcove where the double Dutch jump rope destroyer girls had beat the shit out of her, trying to steal her lunch money.

Itchy shocked her back into the here and now with a dab of isopropyl to her inner thighs. She had paid cash for the abortion. She was working part time as an analyst at a microchip plant. If she stayed there for one year, she'd be eligible for health coverage, get a plan that offered anonymity, blue chip prescription drugs, airy waiting rooms, customer service on speed dial. For years, check-ups had been a fantasy. Bankruptcy loomed with every middle of the night creek and tremor and mysterious spot on her body that sent her to the clinic in a hypochondriac stupor; liv-ing on pins and needles each day for news that she wasn't dying. Now, after bills, rent, food, and gas, she had enough to coast for a month before the worry crept in, drinking in the glittering season of cloudless days when she got off work. It had been the longest stretch of no rain, the bane of brown lawns and dusty reservoirs, a sloppy kiss to restless animals and Jehovah's Witnesses sounding the call of apocalypse.

She was an on-the-cusp Cancer. Cancer's horoscope said not to wait on big decisions like quickie abortions. When she was riding the bus to work, she read horoscopes over people's shoulders. Zeroing in on Cancer and that of whoever she happened to be fucking at the time. In her mind, Cancer's horoscope said the sooner she could get the abortion done and get back to her job, the better. So she pushed the fast-forward button when the intake counselor lilted on about options, brochures, deliberation.

When she got to the clinic, a bony white man with an Operation Rescue placard skulked like a smashed polecat around the entrance. He squeezed a yellow tennis ball in his left fist, looking over his shoulder every second for invisible co-conspirators, beanstalk legs jammed onto hip bones straight from the Pleistocene. She saw a Datsun hatchback a few yards away with phrase, *The meek shall inherit the earth* spray-painted in gold on the bumper. A terrier panted forlornly out of the back window. If the polecat was there when she finished, she'd give him a love letter about how the pregnancy fuck was interstellar. One in a billion among all the fucks in all actual and possible galaxies since the dawn of time. First on the list of things that kept her stirring and lupine at 4 a.m., trying not to reach for a cigarette. Adrift in racing thoughts on what particular soup of molecules had collided to form her. One millimeter off and she would've been a scorpion lurking under a rock, a cow chewing cud, a porcupine. She'd learned in science class that everything was random. No harmony, rhyme, or reason to the downward march of seconds that pushed bodies forward into the earth's mass grave.

Itchy peered down at her from his antiseptic mask, head bulbous amid the heavens of halogen lights. She'd grab the polecat, shave his privates, prep him for birth. Scoop the teeming squadron of cells out of her uterus and build him his own with play dough and a tourniquet. Do a transplant in the back seat of the hatchback with the terrier as her wingman. Put him on lockdown to swim in nine months of shit, pain, barf, woe, and poverty.

When the abortion was done, the nurse swabbed her down, jotted the time on her clinic chart, gave her fifteen minutes to recover, packed her off with a shoulder squeeze and some Tylenol, then bustled off to the next patient.

The street was empty when she went to her car. A pamphlet with a picture of a bloody fetus in a jar flapped under her windshield wiper. Polecat popped out from the Datsun, clutching a stack of pamphlets, watching the clinic door for fresh meat.

She slid behind the wheel and took out a plastic baggy from the glove compartment. The nurse had given her an old, industrial-sized sanitary napkin to absorb the bleeding from the abortion. She reached down and maneuvered it out of her pants, putting it and the pamphlet in the baggy. She pulled up next to the Datsun and shoved the baggy under polecat's windshield wiper.

"Here's something for the cause, brother!" she yelled.

Polecat spun around, dropping his pamphlets as he ripped the baggy off the windshield and held it up to the sun, scowling.

"Bitch! Motherfucking psycho bitch!" He ran after her car in the turn pocket. In the rear mirror, she saw a station wagon barreling toward him. The driver slammed on the brakes, going into a skid before hitting him. He thudded onto the hood. The baggy popped into the air, spiraling free and clear, splattering onto the window of a church van in the opposite lane, the words "Jesus Saves" emblazoned on the side.

Igneous

UNDER THE *CLUNK-BUZZ* OF 1 a.m. TV eruptions, they talked, unpacking the day in sluggish, cul-de-sac sentences. The mother cursed about work shitheads while the father chewed on the price of gas, the ever-exploding light bill, and the neighbors' baying hellhounds, raunchily out for blood behind wrought iron gates.

Since elementary school, the *clunk-buzz* and parents' chatter had been her soundtrack and sedative. The two of them, sparring, watching, sparring, snoring, until one night, a sound—just under a Big Mac jingle—slid soft and slithery from the father's mouth.

"Urboog," he said. The slither turning into a squawk.

An insurance ad had come on, selling bundles for autos, homes, boats, howitzer cannons. She was not sure what she'd heard him say, until the mother repeated it, snickering the knowing snicker of rebuke.

"Urboog?"

There was a moment of silence, punctuated by the refrigerator's hum, the toilet's burble, a robot nightbird trilling all the niggling, fugitive sounds that conspired against her when she went to bed, counting sheep on the knife's edge of wakefulness.

In the morning, at breakfast, she stared down into her bowl of cornflakes and divided them into regiments: Kryptonite vs. gypsum. Stalagmite vs. stalactite. Rat vs. bat. Mother vs. father. Night vs. mare. Igneous vs. metamorphic.

Airplanes roared overhead and dipped in and out of view. The parents sat across from her in their work clothes, listening. Air traffic control had moved the flight path farther to the east. The sounds got closer and closer every week. Kiril was certain the planes would be on top of them soon, shearing off the roof, the pilot and crew peering inside, doing reconnaissance on the ant farm of their apartment.

The parents chattered on about scheduling, workflows, the boil-on-the-butt irritant of discount gulping customers in endless queues at the Swifti-Mart. They'd finally made junior manager and head courtesy shuttle driver after being rank and file for a decade, scoring a seventy-five cent bump from minimum wage, doing overlapping shifts that spat them out onto the streets at 10:45 p.m. sharp. The gibberish of the night before was gone. But she knew what she'd heard. Every time she tried to ask about it, they talked over and through her, scolding her table manners and incomplete math homework, contrasting her nappy hair to the ivory tower cascade of Rapunzel curls sported by the girls on the first floor. Edging her out of the door to the school bus with a pat on the head and a half week's lunch money.

Deciphering the gibberish became a morsel for her to suck on for the rest of the day. She thought about it cowering in the school cafeteria amid jeering food fighting ferrets from eighth grade. Thought about it while dodging creamed corn cups and chicken fried steak. Thought about it and the problem of Veronica, the ace boon wannabe light of her life. Veronica had been shipped out to another school, sentenced to watch paint peel in Sunday church service for the lip-lock she'd given Kiril behind the bungalows, aflush with her first *A* in Algebra.

They'd been spotted and tagged.

"Y'all nasty," the top point guard on the girls' varsity basketball team had said, a heat-seeking missile aiming an imaginary jump shot at them, snitching to the locker room during P.E. at sixth period. This led to a look-at-those-freak-lesbos chant to the tune of "Three Blind Mice."

After Veronica had been banished, there was no one else she could tell about the parents' squawk language, other than her rocks. She kept a collection under her bed. A kingdom that had started when her mother had given her a pair at seven, a gleaming, speck-led duo from the Earth's spinning core. It was the only gift she'd ever been given because the parents said birthdays and Xmas were for sinners. Night after night, the rocks nested there. Confidantes, innocent of the creeping terror of middle school, ever so lucky, ever so loyal. They pledged never to squeal, betray, or snitch through loose lips curdled with picayune drama. She kept one in her pocket on school days, taking refuge in its stillness, the world tumbling around her as she waited for the bus. She whispered commands into it when no one was looking. "Take me away from here. Tell me where you've been. Keep my voice for eternity. Make me inanimate like you. No blood, no feelings, no soft, dirty crumbling bits."

She willed her eyes into burning black holes to blast the fer-rets into subatomic particles.

But nothing moved, nothing changed, nothing flamed. The eighth graders still gnashed their chompers about popping Gila monster pimples, copped feels in the bathroom, pulverized aster-oids in the greasy spoon video game across from the school while fantasy spitballing white teachers in a nuclear flood to the dean's office.

After work, the parents fell into bed with the TV turned up. The wood paneling that separated their rooms vibrated with their gibberish amid police chases, murders, car jackings, kidnappings, fires, crashes, and pet adoption pandemonium from the morning news. It dribbled down to a pinpoint of white noise as she wrig-gled in the seamy grip of REM.

One night, she got out an old tape recorder and hovered by the wall, waiting for the squawks to begin.

If the floorboards creaked… If they heard her…

If they found out she was recording them, would she van-ish in the middle of the night like snot-nosed Willard Jones in apartment 3B? Zapped between sour milk and bedtime cookies and the rainbow test pattern beckoning like a shit God from the banged-up Zenith that only got three good channels when the weather was clear, calm, stuporous?

Snot-nosed Willard had never been heard from again. The space where his body laid replaced by a stuffed animal, a snug as a bug in a rug, glassy-eyed Tigger grinning from underneath the covers of his trundle bed.

She kneeled against the wall, pressing the red "record" but-ton, pushing the vision of Willard from her thoughts. The squawks faded. The tape recorder whir got louder in the bog water silence of the two rooms, shivering against each other like conjoined twins. One of the parents shuffled out of bed to turn off the TV. Would someone go out into the hall to use the bathroom? Launch into an insomniac roam? Make the dreary trek from bedroom to kitchen and back again to kill time? Stare into the bottomless maw of the still dark street and contemplate bailing for good, setting sail down, down, down to the underground, to the stratigraphy of everything that went before?

She strained against the wall and heard nothing but the apnea wheeze of the parents settling back into their bombed-out mattress.

They would be blissfully dead to the world for five hours be-fore they staggered in to work.

She crawled back under the covers and lay still. The smirk of 3B Tigger rose in front of her. She had only seen Willard a few times, heard his cloying voice as he went about smashing Hot Wheels, whimpering about the hotness of the nightly bathwater. a paper doll cutout of random sounds until he went silent. A mes-sage stuffed into a bottle thrown into the sea.

Did Tigger have the same memory as the boy?

She wondered this on the way to school. The tape was secure in her backpack. The rock jiggled in her pocket. She would muster up the courage to play the tape for her life sciences teacher who knew foreign languages, or, at least, claimed to. The teacher roamed the quad and chomped tuna fish during nutrition, extolling the virtues of nematodes to the campus aides zipping by on their go-karts. Kiril thought she could trust her, maybe, partially, because she'd be too obsessed with the inner worlds of squirmy creatures, too indifferent to higher life forms to rat Kiril out to her parents or the principal.

After school, Kiril waited for the other kids to leave, then approached Tuna with the tape, tongue-tied, watching her stamp *F*s onto a pile of pop quizzes in rapid fire.

"This thing is in bad shape," Tuna grunted, pressing down the play button on the chunky classroom tape recorder. "They're delicate animals, these things. Tapes, that is. Once had a job splicing them for a record producer. Eight hours a day in a basement with no lunch. Had to identify any offending material and snip it, sew it up, and make it sound like it'd never been there… Can barely hear anything. Are you sure this is what you wanted me to listen to?"

Kiril nodded. She had never had a full-blown conversation with Tuna, avoiding eye contact when her name was called or homework was returned or lab partners were assigned in plodding alphabetical order.

"I recorded it through the wall," she muttered, kneading her creamed corn-stained T-shirt into a knot. At two minutes in, the squawks sounded, crisp as forest leaves crunching underfoot.

Tuna sat up straight on the stool. "They're plotting something," she said.

"How do you know?"

"By the cadence of their voices."

"Cadence?"

"Tempo. Pace."

"How can you tell they're plotting by that?"

"Deduction. Why else would they be talking nonsense in the middle of the night? How long has this been going on? Why didn't you confront them on it?"

"Dunno. Maybe a week."

"Where do your parents work?"

"At the Swifti-Mart, managing stuff, driving the shuttles."

"Place is a rip-off. Fruit's packed with pesticides, and they got us Negroes doing all the peon jobs. Wouldn't shop there if my life depended on it." She jammed the speaker up to her ear. "You live near the airport? Sounds like planes in the background."

In her dreams that night, she was falling upward and being sucked into tentacles of orange sky-shooting lava. The brains who sat in the front of Tuna's class and aced every exam watched from the ground, twirling in a dust storm, chanting in a mishmash of English and the parents' squawk speak. She woke up to the sound of doors shutting and piss in her pants, the alarm clock frozen at five sixteen. If she was late for school, the brains would be converging on her empty seat on the bus. Once, one had squeezed her butt cheek like a toy horn. She'd yelled out to the bus driver, but the woman barely cut her eyes in the rear mirror before shifting back to traffic.

"They cram their junk into Jordaches two sizes too small. What do they expect? They shake their stripper pole asses down the aisles. What do they expect? Lie down with dogs, and get up with fleas. What do they expect?" she overheard the women drivers saying, comparing their hellion cargo on a smoke break.

Lying under the busted alarm clock, pieces of ceiling plaster sprinkled down on her hair from the upstairs neighbors' marathon holy roller hollering. She could barely move her legs, arms swimming in robot claws at her sides. She willed the claws to shrink, then sat up and went to the bathroom to wash off. The parents' voices bounced through her head, ripping her for being tardy, smelly, messy. Everything that a Tigger could never be, wise behind its cold, hard, downward spiral eyes. The tape recorder loomed in a silhouette on her desk. It had been pried open. The tape spooled onto the floor in brown garlands, a heap big enough to hide a small body. She unraveled it, bracing herself, half expecting to find the boy from 3B there cowering at the sight of her robot claws.

Had the parents listened to the tape while she was sleeping, swapped it, or sabotaged it, afraid of exposure?

The phone rang. A secretary buzzed in pastel tones on the other end. The parents had not come in to work. A sub had to take over her father's courtesy shuttle route. Did she know where they were? Was there another adult in the house she could speak to? Kiril shook her head, forgetting for a moment that the secretary couldn't see her. She gripped the black receiver, fumbling for her voice, croaking "no" as the building vibrated with the mass exodus of bodies launching to work, school, the laundromat.

"Tell them to give HQ a call if they surface, sweetie," the secretary said, ringing off in a cloud of white lady pity. Kiril counted to ten, then went to the parents' room. The bed spread gleamed in beige pressed perfection. Nary a wrinkle, muss, imprint, or betrayal of their presence. The dresser swam with costume jewelry, gnarled receipts, multicolored pills, cigarette packs, Juicy Fruit wrappers, and photo negatives. She picked one up and held it to the light, flinching at the sight of herself, face turned inside out, frame by frame; she was a doppelgänger, sitting at the window of the school bus, hunching alone on the quad with her lunch on her lap, plodding home, the brains trailing her in the background, heads down, immersed in their brain babble.

At school later that morning, she sat in Tuna's class and waited to show her the negatives. Tuna passed out the weekly quizzes in military order, highest grade to the lowest, watching the brains marinate in smugness with each fail.

"Remember, the meek and the humble shall inherit the earth," she said after the last paper had been snapped up, and Kiril crumpled her bloody C- under the desk before the boy behind her could talk shit and boost his brownie points with the brains. He burped instead, cutting a mushroom cloud path of destruction through the jeering class. The door opened and a school resource officer walked in. She scanned the rows. Tuna jolted to attention, disdain flickering in her sandpaper eyes. The inner sanctum of the room was breached.

Kiril's name was being called over the loudspeaker. Burp boy giggled and chanted, "Kiril rhymes with virile." He licked his lips with pride as the officer thumped him on the shoulder to be quiet and motioned for Kiril to follow her.

"C'mon," she said.

"Why?" Kiril asked. The officer grunted, whisking her down the rain dappled hallway festooned with Doritos bags. She squeezed the tape in her pocket, ignoring the titillated your-ass-is-grass gawks from the open classroom doors. The officer guided her through a side gate to a waiting squad car.

"What did I do?"

"Get in," the woman said, opening the back door. The vice principal had emerged from his cubbyhole in the main office to oversee her eviction from campus, awash in geysers of sweat, walkie-talkie pressed to his pale dripping ear. A fleet of Swifti-Mart courtesy shuttles rumbled past with blacked-out windows. She turned, craning to see if her father was driving one. The officer guided her into the backseat, slammed the door, and lurched behind the wheel. They peeled off after the shuttles. The police radio blared reports about toilet bombs, truants jumping fences. A few units were being dispatched to the airport for an aerial show.

"Did you talk to your parents this morning?" she asked.

"They were gone when I woke up."

She squinted at Kiril in the rear mirror. "Where's the tape?"

"What did they do?"

"Give me the tape and the rock."

"I don't have a tape or a rock."

"Liar."

Kiril moved her hand over her pocket. The rock jutted from the seams. If the woman rushed her, she would be ready. "I'm not."

The windshield wipers thudded back and forth as the officer watched her in the mirror.

"I need them for safekeeping."

"Not a liar."

"There's this story they tell about a wooden boy named Pinocchio. Nose grew long every time he lied."

"What did they do?"

"You mean, what did *you* do. Quit playing dumb. You dumped them and shared the tape with an outsider. We can't, we won't allow it."

The officer's eyes narrowed to slits. A car hydroplaned up ahead. The first Swifti-Mart shuttle swerved to avoid it, veering onto the shoulder. Its front door flew open. As they passed, Kiril saw the heads of stuffed Tiggers poking up from the high-backed seats.

"My father drives one of those," she said.

"Fuckup," the officer said.

"What?"

"He's a fuckup. Both of them. Father driving like a fucking maniac, mother letting herself get sucked into management. Got too complacent. And you, letting that asswipe hear the tape and try to decipher it—"

"Turn around. I-I want to go back and see if it's him."

"Do you really?"

Kiril hesitated. The slits darkened, whirring with the *clunk-buzz* of a distant universe. She closed her eyes, wanting to unsee the stuffed animals, to unhear the officer's rants and their oddly familiar cadence, the message humming beneath her words; not quite English, not quite gibberish, but the same color and shape as the parents' tape-recorded voices.

The officer looked up at the sky. Planes moved between the rain clouds. "Give me the rock, you coward," she sneered, switching stations, turning the volume down. Static crackled, a flatlining hiss like the undertow of waves cracking apart a boat from stem to stern, then, gently, the unintelligible squawk she'd heard from behind the parents' wall lilted from the speaker.

"Bloody, Christ. We're late." The officer turned on the siren and maneuvered around the stopped cars. Rubberneckers fidgeted at the stoplight, flowing out from the liquor store and the laundromat under crooked umbrellas, snapping Polaroids in super slo-mo. The Tiggers gaped mockingly out at them from the back window.

"I can only drive so fast," the officer said into the radio. "Airport's five minutes away."

Kiril sat up in her seat. "Airport! What? Why are we going there?"

She had been to the airport once, on a day trip to watch the planes take off and land. Drinking vending machine orange soda and eating potato chips, stealing a Continental airlines pin from the lunch pail of a little white boy. The parents had left her at the window and gone to browse in the gift store. Outside, planes launched into the void, breaking the black sky. She'd watched until they'd vanished completely, wondering if they were going to the time before the planet was born, if there were flesh and blood passengers onboard or just holograms of real people. She followed them until her eyes hurt. The second she stopped concentrating, she could make one fall out of the air—baby bottles, suitcases, overhead bins raining down on the terminal. Then her mother came back with souvenir "pet rocks" from the gift shop. A gag instruction booklet was taped to the front of the package, murmuring, "Take me away from here. Tell me where you've been. Keep my voice for eternity. Make me inanimate. No blood, no feelings, no soft, dirty crumbling bits."

What was that now?

Squawks bleated from the police radio, speeding them through the terminal. Slowly, they became an alphabet, crowding out the English words that had ruled her every waking moment. The other language flooded back to her, the dark curl of water from the womb lapping at her feet, rising to her knees, coming to the rescue.

The officer looked up at the sky, then at her watch. "The fighter jets have ten minutes before the humans attack. They're waiting for your command, captain. Snap the fuck out of it. If you're not going to do your job, I will—" She stopped the car in the middle of the street, lunging at Kiril, squawking in a voice like her mother's, snickering the knowing snicker of rebuke she'd heard in the mornings under the TV.

Kiril touched her shoulder blades, certain there were feathers sprouting, willing them not to fail her as she kicked the door open, ran into the crowd, and put the rock to her mouth, uttering a command to the planes overhead listening for her signal.

"Urboog," she squawked.

The planes dove, igneous rocks raining from the cargo holds and onto the seething ant farm of travelers below.

"Urboog!" she repeated, adjusting her mouth to form the English syllables under her breath. "Destroy!"

Little Surfer Boy

THEY LOOK OVER THEIR SHOULDERS before they take to their boards. Watch for the girls huddled in Juicy Fruit gum popping reverie; the kids beating sandcastles into corn mush; the butt-cheek flashing old-timers settling down for a snooze under big yellow umbrellas. They steady themselves, then take flight, working the waves into submission. Salt clogs their noses, mouths, eyes, thrusting them into blindness, into the watery graves they'd been dreaming of, been memorizing from the first time they had learned to surf as small boys enraptured with the rip curl gods.

They watch for cues from Jake, rising imperially from the water in a Neptune arc with his suction cup feet steadied on the board like some kind of evolutionary marvel, like some kind of special dispensation from the Lord. Our Jake holds the record for staying up the longest before the waves smack him down on his ass. He is a lecher exhibitionist, toying with each little ripple in the ocean divinely served up to him in a neat tiny bow. Lucky fuck had never had his neck twisted and wrung out trying to execute. Lucky fuck was delivered into this world by a midwife with a fistful of Mr. Zog's easing him out of the womb. His bull-necked royal highness, all bee-stung lips and hot steroid lust. We creamed to see him sucking his stomach in all concave and shit in the weight room mirror when he thought no one was looking while he smacked fair Wilson on the ass with a wet towel.

They watch for the shoreline audience. Male surf groupies arrive on foot, spilling from the streetcars that dammed up at the beach terminus every hour, leaning out of cars idling for some-place decent to park. Wolf packs dodge the bruised roller-skating legions of little girls and chop through the dregs of June gloom on this first day of summer.

And Jake's crew liked that stretch of beach because the wave span was neatest. The elemental Milky Way glide of paranormal orbit in the split-second suspension between air and water was just right. The sandcastle mushers keep score with their shovels. The butt-cheek snoozers shake their domino bags for the next game. The sweet sixteens talk crazy about the crews' bodies in 3-D reconnaissance detail.

They could stay out all summer, basking in twenty four-seven, wall-to-wall seaweed funk. None of them have jobs except for Wilson, that white trash fucker bussing tables like a "fucking slave," Jake had snickered. He was the newly minted breadwinner for his mother, laid off from her nursing job as his father rode off into the Akron sunset for fresh pipefitter leads. Only Wilson had regular money in his pocket. The crew bums it off him for cigarettes and rubbers and all-you-can-eat hoagies dripping with cheese from the boardwalk stand. It is the last teenaged summer they can do this shit and have it still be considered cool, shuffling between bouts of community college and applications to Del Taco. The last gasp of the day is hanging around Jiffy Lube for the chance of an opening if ambition hits them. June, July, August was theirs to waste with grand abandon, spreading the seed of the crew all over town, tag-ging their handle in the beach bathroom, the basketball court, the trash barrels in the sand, staging sloppy drunk pantomimes over the mugs of the surfers' pantheon painted on the laundromat wall.

It was Wilson who noticed it first. The shoreline inched up to the street. The arcade, pub, and the laundromat whited out. Buildings swallowed up in a slow procession of open-top cars. Toy

Model *A*s honking, strung together by a child's hand. Wannabe flapper girls with rhubarb-colored arms peeking out of full-body swimsuits and bullet caps. Big band swing music blaring from 78rpm records. Passengers spilling out of the streetcars to catch a glimpse of Manhattan Beach's new revelation-between-the-waves, rising and falling, melded to his board as he adjusted his goggles. The other boys having swum ahead to catch the warm smack of mega surf that came in late afternoon on the night of a full moon.

He paddled, coasted, paddled, coasted, ignoring their sass about how chicken shit he was for hanging back, lacking proper reverence for the moonlight. He'd begun to drift south, his board resisting, bucking up under him, shoving him into the water headfirst. He sank, then burst back to the surface, yelping. The board floated ahead of him, mocking.

He saw a hand grip the board. Then a girl's head rose slowly from the water. She hoisted herself up, lying on her stomach as the waves washed over her. She paddled expertly with both hands, ignoring him as he struggled to get a clearer view. The waves calmed, and she kneeled, bracing herself, listening, rigid with the same watchful posture he'd assumed a thousand times, waiting for the right moment to stand up on the board. The crowd roared, and she stood up. She was taller than him by a few inches, sliding into the snaking furl-unfurl motion of fresh surf, trying to establish her center of gravity before the next torrent hit.

The girl looked out into the swamp of white faces and calculated how long it would take her to get to the other side of the beach to the new Negro resort rippling in the distance like a desert mirage.

Her name was Lizzie, short for Elizabeth. A sound sucked in and spit out with disdain by the neighborhood gremlins who thought she thought she was hot shit; being the only one on the block who knew how to surf.

But yeah, that's right, she *was* hot shit. Hot shit ruling the board in the new sailor striped bathing suit she'd been barred from trying on in the inferno of a Memphis department store the summer before college. The same suit she'd lived in for five hours in 1927 after the pigs pulled her out of the water in Manhattan Beach, California. A platoon of them throwing her in jail sopping wet for swimming with the whites and Asians and Mexicans they said would be contaminated by an errant Negress. Nineteen and a trespassing public menace, according to the official police report. The city getting fat and rich with all the penalties and fines it stole from Negroes.

She started out practicing on a chewed up wooden board in her bathtub. Tearing through a makeshift kiddie pool in the backyard. Wobbling, straightening, perfecting her stance. Dreaming of Duke, the Hawaiian master she'd glimpsed when he first came to California; wanting to be him, stalking the ocean on the Olo board he'd built from scratch.

Looking past the white swamp, she imagined the resort waiters would be serving lunch right about now in April fresh uniforms. She licked her lips at the thought of Cornish hen chickens, pot roast, sirloin downed with iced tea or lemonade, topped off with cobbler, banana pudding, sweet potato pie, or a chocolate sundae. Delicacies she'd lusted after when she was alive, and the first world war bared down on them with hidden fangs.

When Willa Bruce bought the beachfront property with a third of her savings, the butterfly swarms of 1912 had started to die down. The stragglers followed her and Charles clear out to California, acting as menace and protector. Their migratory patterns disrupted by the torrid summer, blood running in the streets, Negro office buildings burned down to bone and toothpicks. She piled their jalopy sky high and told Missouri, *Kiss my Black ass, and deliver me to Canaan*; speeding with one hand on the wheel and the other on her shotgun, grinding through fields of crusty, dusty butterfly wings.

She'd read about the parcel of land being so-called set aside for Negro bidders by a businessman named Peck, a speculator playing great white father from his pulpit of stocks and bonds, the wind of Grand dragons at his back. She didn't want their table scraps. Had had a vision of building her own private beach compound since she was landlocked below the Mason-Dixon. Knee high to the belly of a grasshopper and chewing up the almanac plotting intercontinental expeditions; teddy bears, baby dolls, her first mates and co-captains. Loyalists who wouldn't squeal.

The locals packed the Pacific Electric "big red cars" to go to the Bruce resort on weekends. Migrants trickled in from small tumbleweed towns and big cities. Schoolteachers, clerks, stenographers, letter carriers, dry cleaners, insurance claim underwriters, custodians, doctors, bus drivers; wanderlusters chiseling paradise from the snap of gray waves, the sky bleeding into the ocean at dusk, jonesing for a taste of the Pacific just beyond the bullwhip gaze of white people.

On opening day, Bruce had twenty reservations. If that number held steady, she could break even. If it doubled, she could turn a profit. Use the proceeds to build a chain of resorts, Negro strongholds along the coastline for as far as the eye could see. Bullet, gas, and bomb-proof. Bunkers stocked with a year's worth of essentials. God had said Satan would go up in flames in Armageddon. White America and its itty-bitty zygotes nipped in the bud before they had the brain cells to form a genocidal thought. Neutralized before

111

the tender grasp of a lynching rope. She woke up in a hot flash flood every midnight with the same plan. Eye for an eye. Tooth for a tooth. Marooned in a recurring dream where she was rowing a boat down the empty shore. Lured by warm lights dancing in the distance. An inn with the softest beds, the cleanest spic and span rooms. Parlors buzzing with debate and rumination. Apocalypse could rage around them and nothing would penetrate. A paradise eked from the sweat of her back and the stroke of her pen.

The first guests came in on the Friday after the Titanic sank. Gorging on the sunsets and pristine surf, squirreling away home-made teacakes for later, taking bets on the number of survivors from the cruise ship. Newspaper headlines screamed that over one thousand were feared dead. Publicly, Willa lamented. Privately, she dismissed it, saying to Charles, "Better them than us. They burned us out of Springfield, mauled us like dogs in Atlanta, set their savages on us down in Wilmington, and where were the boo hoos of half the planet then?"

He could only swim so long before he drowned. Pelicans bleated overhead in conspiracy. Quizzical, amused. He'd always been fascinated by their jutting beaks and dinosaur eyes, but now he resented their every move. The freedom in the way they glided and swooped with supernatural ease, taking their time, calculating which fish to pluck from the water. He yelled out for the girl to give him back his board, but only a toad's croak came out. A tidal wave choking him, like the evil side of him was rising up from his throat to get revenge on the elements. He could see Black kids with buckets digging sand castles on shore, sporting striped one-piece bathing suits, relics from an old busted newsreel. If he could morph into being one of them. Be a body snatcher from that seventies movie that had scared him shitless in reruns. Ask God's forgiveness for wanting someone else to die in his place. And if there was really nothing up there, nothing claiming dominion in the sky, nothing watching over the earth, nothing but being born, living, and dying, all in the millisecond of a mite's fart, then, fuck it, there'd be no forgiveness to ask.

What Elizabeth wouldn't have given for the sweet surrender of chocolate. So sweet you were liable to get diabetes just looking at it, a river of it glistening from one of Willa Bruce's notorious, terrorist to the tongue hot fudge sundaes. The Bruce resort served the best sundaes for miles around. The perfect ratio of vanilla ice cream to hot fudge, to whipped cream, to nuts. Sundaes and lol-lygagging and mornings that melted into nights in a blur of freeze tag and hide 'n' seek and sand crab hunting were the hook, line, and sinker that kept the kids clamoring to come back summer after summer, shorn of responsibility, nursing secret crushes; boy to boy, girl to girl, girl to boy.

When she died, there had been no flashing revelation, no cher-ubs singing, no beating of black wings.

She was alone, watching the white boys on their boards, stunted in the majesty of their sand grain existence.

She powered forward on the stolen board.

No trumpets, dark tunnels, fire or brimstone, no ferry men to take her over to the other side.

She reveled in seeing the resort kids taking turns making sand angels, some scurrying before the tide came in, some stay-ing down on their backs to feel the surf wash over them. Blissed out on the grand illusion of being footloose and fancy free as the town fathers plotted against every beam and plank in the Bruce's building at their church services and garden parties; women, chil-dren, and Fido in tow to join in the festivities.

And, still, there was the matter of the chocolate fudge reward waiting for them after braving the dares. Drizzled over the perfect dollop of vanilla ice cream to calm their fears about being ripped as butt ugly, pigeon toed, shit-breathed, tar babyish. The underdogs tried to one-up the popular kids to keep from getting their asses handed to them first, playing the dozens until the emptiness in the pit of their stomachs settled down just a little. If she could make it to the shore in time, she could stop it all. Blaze right through the gawking white boys circling in the water, snap up the bullied and bruised, and ride to infinity.

If it really existed. And what exactly would they do there after every possible world had been exhausted? Melt down and become one of the billion unclassified creatures at the bottom of the sea. Go back to the gelatinous stew of the time before birth.

She steadied herself on the board and pushed on.

His goal was to move up to one of the oil change jobs at the lube place. Your candy ass should at least know how to change oil in a car, his uncle had told him. He was planning everything out by year. The program was to have his own apartment by twenty-one, get his girlfriend a ring, buy his own wheels and pay his own car insurance, settle into a good rhythm for the next six years. He broke things down into even increments, methodical since his first glimpse of daylight, his first taste of power, collecting pennies from the kitchen floor and storing them in his mouth to make his mother crazy. He liked to believe he was more than average, had done things according to plan, not jerked off, not smoked pot, not violated curfew, not let himself be led by the nose by temptation; resisted, so strongly, the urge to peel his little cousin with a paring knife and see whether his mixed-breed blood was the same as pure white blood. These goblin "creepings" that overcame him when he was waiting in line, washing the dishes, watering the lawn, muting the volume on one of his father's tantrums to a simian mumble. The bargaining began in his head as he dropped the seeds of repentance for every mental transgression he could remember. Not fucking now, when he had just begun to get shit organized, just formed a sense of personal mission. "Not fucking now," he whispered, his forearms burning from trying to stay afloat as he watched the girl bob and weave in the sun's halo, almost to the shore. The scene shifted, and instead of the Model As and flappers and swimmers writhing to Big Band, he could just make out his car in the parking lot, the vinyl top gleaming amidst the other Detroit beaters. He'd spent the last two dollars of his allowance on the parking fee. Scraping nickels from between his car seats while the runty parking attendant took the money, put the ticket on his window, and blathered on about litter, pollution, shark sightings, the paradise of crystal clear waters when he'd seen Duke, the surfing legend, as a pup in 1912.

"Back in the day, we could lay out right up on here, let our boners cool," he said, pointing to the blacktop with a wizened half digit, cheek bulging with snuff to calm his jitters. He'd lost part of his index finger in an accident assembling a Molotov cocktail. Dropped out of aviation school to live on the beach at nineteen. No future, no plan other than to sleep, eat, shit, surf, wipeout, rinse, and repeat. Joined the secret army of upright community men patrolling the coast from dawn to dusk. Melted into the pride of Ivy League captains of industry and law enforcement and philanthropy and oil and retail, all dedicated to a single purpose. Even though he was branded cracker trash out of Lawndale, he could hold his head high being a foot soldier. His special skill was pyrotechnics, knowing the physics of fire, wind shear, direction, burn rate. The only thing in the world he'd mastered. Setting him apart from the other middling atom sacks roaming the planet born at the exact same time and day. He believed that everyone

115

had a cosmic twin, an invisible ball and chain weighing them down, junk noise just behind their eardrums, sonar in the brainstem. The twin moved parallel in dream fragments, stalking roads not taken. Starting fires gave him the illusion of control. Freed him from the crushing taint of ordinariness. Away from the ghost twin and its designs, toward his own destiny. That brilliant blue morning among his fellow patriots, chanting "Thy will be done, on earth as it is in heaven," while the last Colored bathhouse went up in smoke like God intended.

"Consider yourself lucky, son," he told Wilson. "We sacrificed so you could twiddle your thumbs, chase tail, get high, and play Peter Pan every summer."

Flailing in the water, Wilson called out for the old man but his voice was even weaker, swallowed up by pipsqueak cheers bouncing off metallic waves, pocked with oil and flotsam, gristle from the Titanic. Saltwater stung his nose, flooding his throat, his eyes, every gaping mortal orifice. And as he looked up one last time before going under, he saw that the thief who'd stole his board had made it to shore, striding through the sand in a sailor-striped bathing suit. She raised his surfboard over her head, greeting the Bruce resort waiters stationed on the veranda. White napkins draped over their arms. Hot fudge goblets glistened out at the children playing tag in the sinking sun, clamoring for their turn on the board.

What a glorious day to be a California girl.

Courier

BEHIND THE WHEEL. THE STREET was brimming over. Five fifteen p.m. I stopped to light a cigarette, watch the cars pass.

One. Two. Three.

They drove in from Exposition Boulevard. Paused at the stop sign on Mulberry. Shark finned machines glinting with steam. Gunboat wonders steered by white men; hatless, ties slung over their shoulders, turkey necks open at the collar, fingers drumming the steering wheel, sandpaper lips whistling lopsided to all the off-key be-bop-a-lulas. Armpits swimming in the 100-degree heat.

It was Mulberry this week. Nutmeg the week after. Maple the week after that. My heart thrummed, hyped up, hot as shit at the prospect, the streets damming up sleepily in my head.

Five thirty p.m. I watch as a streetcar rolls in from Venice. Blink, and the tracks fill with school kids swinging their lunch pails. Blink, and gaggles of white women amble past, pushing towheaded urchins in strollers. Blink, and gum grinding white girls barrel through, comparing new 45s from the downtown record store.

Would be fun to be a deejay broadcasting deep down from a bullet hole in Middle America's head. Polluting the world. Spilling its secrets. Purging all the rot and chaos. The theft of every Delta blues guitar hook spilling from between its yellow teeth.

I finished my cigarette and stubbed it out in the ashtray, parked in front of 2508 Mulberry, shut off the engine, flopped back on the pleather seat and waited.

In my rear mirror, I saw him. The next one. Buck-toothed boy spinning a football in the air, ginger tendrils spilling over his forehead. I'd emptied a dozen of them into my engine. Would soon be able to power my whole fleet.

California Dreamin'.

I started up the engine again. Watched the boy's face crater as he drew his arm back and shot the sweetest pass into the air.

I run a courier service in L.A. County. Five guys, five cars. Ex-cons, drifters, insomniacs. I'm fucking one of them on a semi-regular basis. A rookie driver named Mallard Kennedy who used to be in my zoology class at the community college I taught at. Dreamboat Mallard is older and more persnickety than the other students, head in the clouds, tuned out to the muck of the real world, gorging on surf punk on his Walkman and White Castle in his corroded Flintstones lunch pail. Blasé about his grade. Blasé about breathing. White boys got it that way. He came to my office hours a few times and hung around, moping, talking doomsday shit about planets colliding, exploding. Said he had pet ferrets that kept him tapped in to the exoplanets. Knew somehow that I had a soft spot for Chordata phylum intelligence. Shared my hankering for the funk of expiring animals. The demon moments between being alive and lurking oblivion. *Shit's perverse right, prof?* he said. But the heart wants what it wants, and we wanted the last throes of semi-dead meat and little pieces of each other thrown into the deal.

I live at the foot of the Santa Monica I-10 freeway offramp near La Brea Avenue and Adams. The first building you see skidding down the exit. Got it in foreclosure from a psycho fuck lottery ticket seller, Pentecostal cult preacher at the end of Reagan-Bush. Lying in the darkness, I see Kennedy's boots on the floor by the foot of the bed. He snores, whinnies, turns. Ferret fur under his stumpy nails. I hired him after he failed my class. Admin suspected him of calling in a campus bomb threat after Gore got cheated out of the election in 2000. DNA and surveillance video could never prove his guilt. I wanted a ghost genius like that on my team. A ferret whisperer who could beam us out into the subarctic nuclear winter of infinity. Deliver a package in under warp speed. Matter moved and deposited before you even knew you needed it. Before you even thought it. Before you or your mama, grandmama, or great grandmama were even born. A package could wind up on a seventeenth century plantation in Wilmington, Delaware, North Carolina, explode, wipe out half the joint, rearrange the molecules that might've been your ancestors, and you'd be born a sixteenth of who you were now or less than the circumference of an aphid's butthole. While Kennedy whinnied, tossed, and turned, I sat up thinking, fantasizing about it, drawing up aspirational intergalactic maps and charts and coordinates.

Strategic deliveries were one way to cure the cancer of the past. I was working on a fuel source that could take the fleet around the County and back. But already we were getting liquefied by the Internet. Out of the ashes, three things would be constant. Dogs. Cockroaches. Rats.

Hell would be being stranded on an Aegean Sea island ruled by regiments of all three. The dogs taking orders from the cockroaches lorded over by the rats camped on by the ticks in a downward spiral of crossbreeding. In my zoology world, all animals weren't created equal. I was partial to missing links, fuzzy mammals, nothing that skittered, squeaked or overbred in the bowels of train stations. That ruled out Homo sapiens. At any time of the day, I could see dogs sniffing around the offramp through my bedroom window. Dobermans circling around torched transmissions, tongues dragging the ground in a surf of tires, bloated hubcaps, air freshener trees slopping onto the street in a big black feral milkshake. No matter how many calls to sanitation I made to get it cleaned up, it was still the same swamp pit. Screeching Muzak after they put me on hold. A recorded message about plastic containers. A recorded message about holiday closures. A recorded message about chemicals it was a felony offense to dump. More ear bleeding Muzak. Schmaltz strings forcing thoughts of mayhem until Kennedy put me out of my misery with his tongue.

I was chasing down a garbage truck, stumbled on one of my drivers getting a blowjob when I found Mulberry. UPS was on strike. For two weeks, a window of opportunity busted open for little outfits like ours. Phone rung off the hook. I could barely keep the tanks full. Happy days were here again. But the ramp shit just kept raining down on my driveway.

I figured I would slip the garbage man a few dollars to swing back and collect it, but my Benjamins weren't big enough. He just looked at them and shrugged, muttered he was a shop steward and what kind of impression would that give if the rank-and-file brothers found out he went dirty. And, besides, didn't I know every rig had a surveillance camera planted by management under the driver's seat? No amount of coaxing could pry him off his high horse. Gave me the finger and rolled out into the blood orange sunrise blasting the Stylistics, the lead's falsetto soaring over a week's worth of amalgamated trash.

I headed north, trying to escape it, its primordial gradations, the memories of every house, apartment, and lean-to within a block's radius compressed in the trail of stink, awash in the subdivision's invisible skin cells. Awash in every niggling little moment of their niggling little lives. Again, gods were bullshit 'cause how could your head not explode trying to keep track of each petty human cesspit cartoon? I rolled up the windows, held my nose, driving with one hand. Motherfuckers honking at me for going slow. Out of the corner of my eye in the street's cul-de-sac, I saw a schlub in a two-toned minivan nodding behind the wheel in slo-mo. It was Manny for Manfred, one of my newer drivers, began most of his sentences in the negative, bragged that he slept on a bed of lotto tickets. One of these days, he was gonna hit it big, he said, clone himself, start a deep space colony.

Big plans radiating from a pea brain. Good heart, pea brain. Always a trade-off with these head-in-the-cloud jaw jackers.

Now there he was, getting serviced in broad daylight. Transported into deep space with his dick on fire while my other boys were tearing up and down the freeways delivering meds, meals, and a shoulder to cry on to shut-ins with no kin. I stopped, wavering on whether I should crash the party or drive on, cut him loose later when the demand for deliveries died down. I was picking up interference from his radio. A Lorelei lure, blasting sour notes over the cookie-cutter frame houses peeking out from the click-clacking railway tracks, and I could see the resident white boys huddled together in mix matched football jerseys living for the double-triple dare of jumping off rooftops to see who was biggest, baddest, hardest. Freckle-faced marauders, bored, counting down until the rump roast feasts in front of the tribe's brand new black and white Zenith. Summertime and the living was easy.

That's how I found Mulberry. Not sure if I was awake or asleep when I did. Not sure if I'd been sucked under the rumble of racing tow trucks massing on the freeway shoulders in the darkness, jonesing for the latest crash. Not sure if I'd found the pot of gold at the end of the rainbow, awakening in a squall of pillow slobber, five hours older and closer to the end of it all. Five hours of certified shuteye was a marathon compared to my miserable three.

A street stuck deep in the vinyl grooves of 1956, needle scratching, dragging over the same canned lyric. When darkness fell and the world around it pulsed with forward movement, chatter about what the next day, week, month would bring. With births and murders and shuffling off to school and punching clocks and doing laundry and waiting at the mailbox for a late county check, watching paint peel and cookies crumble and fires burn. Amid that grind, there was Mulberry, nesting in the void of a football spiraling through the air.

Ginger had some big hands on him. Could catch any pass that came at him. Burping *hut, hut, hut* just to get a cheap laugh, fit in, all nervous and antsy and trying not to shit his pants after the three cheeseburgers he stuffed down his gullet, alone and bored on a Friday at the local greasy spoon. No Negroes need apply.

I could sit and watch for hours. Patience being a virtue. Consider how long it had taken them to finish the first few cancerous sprigs of the interstate system. From a glimmer in Eisenhower's eye to 24/7 bulldozers to ribbon cutting orgies to the giddy roar of unrelenting traffic. Thirty-five years of knocking down Black block after block, house after house, skeleton after skeleton. Three decades and change of taking the Great migration neighborhoods full of Texas, 'Bama, Mississippi, and Arkansas families down to tumbleweeds.

I stayed glued to the oil futures market. Ear to the ground for any wars or geopolitical disruptions in the Middle East, China, Africa, Russia with its primordial pipelines. Like I said, in five years, the Internet would grind us down to subatomic dust if we weren't ready. It kept me awake, bugging Kennedy for back rubs and buzz feeds with my new vibrator in the middle of the night. Someone somewhere would still need physical shit delivered. Food, water, meds, transplant organs, skin on skin. Non-negotiables that couldn't be reduced to the slop of rearranged molecules. I was working on this formula that could get us anywhere in the County in ten minutes, flat. Recurring dreams of teleportation wormed into my every waking moment. Hibernating on a whale's fin in the Atlantic, hiding from the police at the bottom of a creek. Give you a get out of jail free card at the exact second of violent expiration. Would you take it? Would you risk it? Not knowing where in the fuck you'd land?

I shadowed ginger's burger joint. Watched the cooks negotiate dynasties of grease and sludge teeming with Anaconda-fanged microbes. What was the transit-worthiness of modern animal fat? How many miles could it buy us when petro ran out? Some of the hotshot rich companies were transitioning to electric fleets. No way could I afford that shit when we were always in the red, always fucked, drowning in parking tickets, mechanics' bills, insurance, rent hikes, bad credit, sabotaged by drivers bailing for greener pastures in toner cartridge telemarketing or phone sex.

Every new irritant made me forget things. Small to medium things, like the last two digits of my phone number and which gas stations had free air and water. Medium to big things like Kennedy's birthday and birth year. The profile of his face in my side mirror. The thousandth time he'd cried out his dead brother's name, waking up funky and blinking in the sunlight, trying to figure out where he was, plastered at the foot of the bed. All these hairline fracture memory lapses leading me by the nose to the downward spiral into reptilian oblivion.

The Mulberry boys usually started up a football game after they got home from summer school. Rotating lines of scrimmage on postage stamp lawns. A whole pack of them would roll in on the train around four or five, hair spiked up with beach water. How lucky to be able to take the train from the beach to home. Stalking the aisles, bristling with fraternal heat, a baying mob in soggy dungarees.

Kennedy's brother disappeared one day when he was five or six. Search parties tore through the neighborhood, scouring school yards, churches, bus depots, dumpsters. Anywhere a big strapping boy could slip through the cracks, flirt, fraternize, shape shift, get up to mischief, chaos. At first, K was glad because the brother was

123

a mean shit. Wrestled Kennedy in the grass, teased him about his dick size, cheated in card games, took all the bullying and misery he got out on him and tried to be the golden boy when adults were looking.

The family had a funeral for the brother a year after he'd gone missing. Empty coffin for a near six footer. K had wondered if it really was empty. Had a ventriloquist's dummy been dropped in right after the ceremony, or maybe a dead dog or a sacrificial lamb somebody had stuffed in during last rites before the mourners threw dirt and daisies onto the coffin and it was lowered into the ground?

He wondered crazy shit like that aloud, paralyzed with doubt all these years later. I tried to soothe him. Made every honest effort. Stroking his hair. Muttering that it would be okay when it wouldn't. Cursing the brother for visiting him, torpedoing him from the grave, an earwig nesting under the curl of his eyelashes.

K shuffled through life, ate, slept, grieved in the idling time of red lights. Took up space between my walls, starting all over again at the break of dawn as new destinations rolled in from customers who needed deadbeat dad papers served or exotic beasts handed off to international dealers. I drew the line at drugs, for now. Fuck rotting in jail for crackheads, traffickers, and leeches. There was always some woman who got played by a predator and wound up staring at the end of the universe's gun barrel. Job, kids, prospects, the two nickels she rubbed together just to put food on the table all up in a smoke over a misstep while the dipshit penis who punked her hunted for another warm body.

Which is one of the reasons why I got into this business. Not beholden to nobody nowhere. To nothing sentient or halfway sentient. Survival of the fittest while the time bomb ticks and the wheels fall off. Part of me was lulled into believing that shit when I saw the others on the block I grew up on flail, capsize, vanish without a trace. Part of me loved inhaling the elixir of the exceptional

Negro. It drove me in fallow moments, when the neighborhood motherfuckers who'd crushed me as I stuttered out an order in the cafeteria line floated up again like soap bubble demons. I had enough trouble with my own nemeses, chasing away doubt, elves wielding poison pickaxes to my cerebral cortex. They doubled and tripled when I got stuck on the infinite fuel formula. I fantasized about reaching in and plucking them out. Setting them aflame on the pyre of my blissfully dead parents.

There was comfort in animals, though. A reprieve from the elf babble. I monitored the action around the off ramp, hoping the arcane ways of the animal kingdom would give me a sign. Beasts were the little bellwethers of chaos and entropy. Squirrels, possum, raccoons skittering past, pushed out of their natural habitats by development. Dogs and cats flattened into tomato paste by speeding cars. Bits of them rising up in silent revolt in combustible engines. Every morning, I started herding road kill in the trunk at 4 a.m. when Kennedy was out cold. Boy could stay comatose through nuclear bomb detonations and chainsaw massacres. In another life he was part feline, sleep interrupted by the odd waking moment. For my purposes, he was a reliable alibi. If the jackboot pigs came out of the woodwork while I was on Mulberry, followed me with guns and batons to our perch on Adams Boulevard, K could disarm them, be their milquetoast next of kin with the jug-eared grin. Lie through his teeth for me. If I killed one or two, how many little legacy Nazis from the next generation would never be born? How many bloodlines edited out of existence? How much embryonic blood and guts would go up in smoke, never having the chance to form into a whining, craven, sorry excuse for a human?

The Catch-22 was my engine would only go back there in the buzz of an alternative fuel source. Most of the time, it couldn't do roadkill. I'd drain ramp possum through it, and the engine would click, fake me out, leave me stranded in the hum of the football marauders, the weekend warrior civil servants tinkering on hydrogen bomb replicas in their basements.

After the roadkill failed, I experimented with a few chimps I picked up from a zoo animal black market in Corona. A mother and son duo that started to expire on the dusty 90-minute ride back to the city. I stored them in my classroom for the night. Caught hell from the school administration after a janitor nearly keeled over from the odor.

From there, I worked my way up the great chain of being. Spent some time in the downtown library, looking over census reports from '56. Mulberry, Nutmeg, Maple, and a few other streets that didn't exist anymore had a high concentration of transplants from Michigan, Iowa, Indiana. Assembly line workers who went hog wild with the postwar manufacturing and defense booms that spit out promotions and filthy lucre for white men.

My parents met under the spoke of a plane wheel at McDonnell Douglas Aircraft. Got matching pink slips after Watts had burned to a crisp, and the feds blew their load on commission reports, selling swamp land to the masses. Before the layoffs, they rode the last of the streetcars downtown, ears pricked for jobs, situations, side hustles. Miss Ann needs someone for toilet patrol on Wednesdays. Buffy and Biff are on the hunt for ball boys. Union station shoe shiners, dishwashers, washroom attendants galore. The universe of crapped-on Negro labor that put me through undergrad, then three years of graduate school, clawing my way to a zoology degree they said would never pay for a pot to piss in.

The naysayers had been dead for ten years. Wiped out in a freak electrical storm in Kansas. All I got was a box of miscellany. Dribs and drabs from the last seconds of their lives. Wedding rings, charred underwear, buttons, spare change jangling around. Artifacts as though they'd never been here and I was just a computing error, a colonizer's plant, a fart in the wind. Half of my brain tried to convince me it was true. The other half mourned my parents' absence as I leaned back in the seat, calibrated my breathing to match his, the running boy coming toward me.

Watch him now, galloping, freckled arms pumping at his sides like a dodo bird trying to take flight. Late June, and he's dodging, kicking up grass, screaming, *hit me, hit me, hit me*, practically shitting his pants with excitement about turning nineteen, finally getting his own wheels. Too puny to make varsity, too slow to make JV. But on Mulberry, he was a ginger speed demon, a gridiron giant, showing up all the neighborhood pikers who'd once spat in his face.

I figured he would have the fattest, thickest veins. The prime of Darwinian evolution, anaconda tributaries pulsing with possibility. The kind of veins you could launch a boat in, wind downstream, back to the Revolutionary War, muskets blazing over the Potomac River. Brits promising slaves freedom for sweat, grit, muscle, as his ancestors went to auction for replacements, kiddies jostling in the back of buggies, flush with anticipation.

I sat, invisible, a hunter frozen behind the windshield, guzzling Coke, gnawing at red licorice. I'd do anything other than hard drugs to keep hopped up for the next ten hours. Had to be alert. Had to be primed, or the moment would evaporate, and I'd be back, imprisoned in the slosh of errands run, bills paid, fucks made, a jillion strangers' shit for brains routines exploding all at once on an average ordinary Wednesday in 1999.

I sat, invisible, as he jackknifed a pass to a scowling imp on the sidewalk. Perfect arc. Perfect forearm whip. Sharp enough to have given any of them a buzz cut. He'd be a fine specimen for our needs. A few dozen more and the cost savings could keep us in the black for at least five years. I watched the tangle of sweaty white bodies plow into the rosebush end zone. Traced each player's future on a piece of scratch paper. Took a lighter to it and watched it burn in the ashtray. I wasn't superstitious. There was no god. Nothing beyond the crumbling tip of my nose. Aging

127

to obsolescence by the second. Like the football boys. Counting eternal sheep.

It is Monday, late June, on a lightning in a bottle summer day, and President Eisenhower is set to address the nation about the opening of the shiny new interstate highway. Every TV on Mulberry is fired up and ready to hear him gush about prosperity, the elixir of open roads; how every lane is an ode to national defense, every off-ramp a bulwark against lurking Commies, divine as the Father, Son, and Holy Ghost.

Now, my tank is full to bursting. Sated for the time being. We knock through the county at warp speed. Up the coast, past titanic bonfires, downtown past the dusty trickle of the L.A. River, through the Valley. Past ticky-tacky subdivisions, swap meets, auto junkyards, bowling alleys, greasy spoons, post offices, gas stations, pre-schools hissing with the creak of abandoned swings.

Home looms between night's fingers. As I approach my exit, the ramp is quiet, scrubbed clean. A drooling cocker spaniel limps through the gunk of an old crash, sniffing car parts, Pinto antennae bristling with an end of summer lament from two decades ago. I park, go inside, throw down my keys, snuggle up next to Kennedy in bed. His mouth hangs open, dead to the world again. I lie there for a second, matching his breathing. Up, down. A spiraling football cadence.

"Don't worry, baby," I whisper, smoothing down the tufts of shiny red hair at his temples, breathing in its warm ginger scent. "Don't worry, everything's gonna be alright.

www.ingramcontent.com/pod-product-compliance
Lightning Source LLC
Chambersburg PA
CBHW060741180626
46819CB00001B/62